'Mike, pl...
understand...
talk, but...
I want to as...

'You've lost me,' he muttered.

'I want you to listen to me, then it'll be your turn. This might be forward of me, but I've got to say it. Mike, I love you. I can't imagine loving anyone else, can't imagine loving you more. I love you.'

'And I love you, sweetheart,' he said urgently. 'I love you so much that I—'

'Mike, please stop!' Her voice was high as she interrupted him. 'I'm not sure what you were going to say, and this might be even more forward of me.' She stopped and swallowed, made sure her voice was clear. 'I don't want you to ask me to marry you.'

# DELL OWEN MATERNITY

**Midwives, doctors, babies—
at the heart of a Liverpool hospital**

**Dear Reader**

Of all the departments in a large modern hospital, perhaps the most difficult and most rewarding, must be the maternity section. What responsibility could be greater than knowing that only your skill and training can bring a new life into the world? What thrill could be greater than seeing proud parents carry away the child that you have helped be born?

The three heroines of these books are all dedicated to their work. They are trained in ante-natal, post-natal, delivery suite, SCBU and clinic. They find their careers deeply satisfying. Butthey are also young healthy women, who need further fulfilment outside work.

My three midwives all think they have found love in the hospital—but there are problems. Work and love become intertwined, and it is difficult to sort out priorities, to decide exactly what feelings mean.

Love will always find a way. Our heroines find that that way can be a hard one—but in the end they triumph.

I hope you enjoy reading these stories; I enjoyed writing them.

Best wishes

*Gill Sanderson*

Look out for the next two stories set in
**DELL OWEN MATERNITY**, coming soon from
Mills & Boon® Medical Romance™

# A VERY SPECIAL MIDWIFE

BY
GILL SANDERSON

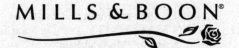
MILLS & BOON®

*MILLS & BOON and MILLS & BOON with the Rose Device are registered trademarks of the publisher.*

*First published in Great Britain 2004*
*Paperback edition 2005*
*Harlequin Mills & Boon Limited,*
*Eton House, 18-24 Paradise Road, Richmond, Surrey TW9 1SR*

© Gill Sanderson 2004

ISBN 0 263 84286 X

*Set in Times Roman 10½ on 12½ pt.*
*03-0205-45049*

*Printed and bound in Spain*
*by Litografia Rosés, S.A., Barcelona*

# CHAPTER ONE

IT HAPPENED the first time that he saw her.

It was a Friday evening, and he was to start his new job promptly on Monday morning at the Dell Owen Hospital. But John Bennet, his new obs and gynae consultant, had suggested that he come to the party at the hospital social club. 'It's for the newly graduated midwives, Mike,' he had said. 'There'll be a lot of the people there that you'll be working with. Meet a few of them informally first. Always a good way to start.'

Mike had agreed with him. He was new to the hospital, new to the district for that matter, and after five years abroad, he felt new to the country. He wanted to get the feel of the place. And after some time at the party he knew he was going to like it. He felt at ease here, as if he was among friends.

For the first hour he had sat at John's table and chatted to other senior members of staff. Then he had decided to mingle. There was dancing to quite a good group—perhaps later on he would ask someone to dance, but first he would just amble around, look at the people he would be working with.

He wasn't a vain man, but he couldn't help noticing one or two interested glances from obviously unattached girls. Well, there were more women than there were partners for them. Perhaps, in a few minutes…

Then he saw her.

At that moment his life altered. He wouldn't have thought that just one glimpse of an attractive face and body could have had such an effect on him. But it did. And he was lost, he had no idea what to do. It was madness, this couldn't be happening to him!

What was he to do? He couldn't just stand and stare at her, he had to have some kind of plan, some means of getting to know her. To give himself time to think, he went to the bar and waited to ask for a glass of wine. And he stared at the mirror behind the bar and, unseen, watched her that way.

When he was given his wine he walked, apparently casually, to stand in the shadow of a pillar and sip his drink. And he looked at her, trying not to be too obvious but unwilling or unable to take his eyes from her. She was gorgeous!

He hoped she wouldn't notice him, see his all too obvious interest. Well, not yet.

She was talking to a small group, a couple of younger women, an SHO and Ellie Crane, a senior registrar he had met who had been sitting at the consultant's table. That would give him the right to walk up to the group, to ask to be introduced. But not yet. For a while he wanted just to look at her.

She was tall for a woman, with raven hair now flowing down to her shoulders. Her dress was a simple grey one. He knew nothing about women's clothes, but this dress seemed rather plain for a party.

But it worked well. The plainness only emphasised the graceful feminine lines of her figure.

And her face! He noted large eyes, a generous mouth—just details. In her face there seemed to be a reserve. There was a melancholy about her, even when she smiled. Some kind of mystery. He knew he had to meet her, find out her story.

Usually, he knew, he tended to be brash. It was a fault. At times he would storm into a situation when waiting and thinking might have been better. But this time he would show more care. Making sure that the girl wasn't moving, he walked back to the consultant's table.

'Everyone's having a good time,' he said, apparently casually. 'People here know how to enjoy themselves. By the way, who's that girl talking to the SHO and the registrar? Have I met her?'

He knew very well that they had never met before.

John shook his head. 'Not yet. But you will. She's one of our stars, belongs half to the local university and half to us. She's the university senior tutor for the midwifery course and she also works on the obs and gynae wards. Moves from one to the other. She's good, dedicated to her job. Her name's Jenny Carson.' John stood. 'Want to meet her? In fact, I've scheduled you to do some lecturing for her. I'll take you over and introduce you.' Then he sat down again. 'Too late. Looks like she's going. She never stays very long at parties.'

Mike watched her saying her goodbyes. He didn't want her to go. He'd seen her, now he wanted to meet her. But he realised there was something else he really had to know. 'Going home to her family perhaps?' he asked, as casually as he could.

'No, not married or anything like that. Apparently no interests apart from work. Concerned solely with her job, dedicated to it. That's the kind of nurse I like. Mary, good to see you!'

Someone else had come to claim the consultant's attention. 'See you in a couple of minutes,' Mike said, and quickly slipped away. He wanted to see this Jenny Carson before she left. They were going to work together so he could introduce himself. He might catch her before she left the building. And if he talked to her he might be able to understand his feelings.

Once or twice Mike had worked high in the Andes, at altitudes where the air was so thin that his heart had seemed to rattle in his chest and it had been difficult to drag in enough oxygen. He had a similar feeling of desperation now.

Jenny decided she was ready to leave. She wasn't a party person, not now. And when she looked at the eagerly gyrating twenty-one- and twenty-two-year-olds, she decided that, at thirty-two, it was time she went.

Of course, she'd had to come. This was the newly graduated midwives' celebratory party, there were girls here she had shepherded over the past four years. She was pleased with their success, quietly proud of her own part in it. She had congratulated everyone, danced with the consultant and a couple of senior members of staff, had politely refused an offer to go out to dinner. But now it was time to go.

For the last five minutes she had been chatting to her two prize students—Lucy Stephens and Maria Wyatt. Both had been offered jobs at the hospital, both had accepted. Jenny was glad. The hospital would benefit from employing them. But now she would leave them to enjoy themselves. Her computer waited, she had work to do.

She picked up her coat from the cloakroom, about to walk out of the club, then she stopped. Just outside was a couple, passionately kissing. If Jenny opened the door she would have to brush right by them. She didn't want to do that, she'd taught the girl and knew she would embarrass her. Jenny sighed. She supposed she could wait a minute.

She didn't hear anyone walk up so it was a bit of a shock when a male voice spoke right behind her. Cheerfully it said, 'Isn't young love wonderful? I wish I were young again.'

A man talking cheerfully about love. This wasn't a conversation Jenny wished to continue. Suspiciously she turned and looked at the man who had spoken.

He was tall, bronzed, a relaxed, easy look to the way he stood. His lightweight grey suit and dark blue, open-necked shirt were casual but elegant. But as Jenny gazed at him, she had another shock. Across his left cheek, from temple to chin, there stretched the whiteness of a scar. The wound that caused it must have been a vicious one indeed. However, it wasn't too disfiguring. But Jenny wondered whether if he wasn't smiling—as he was now—he might look dangerous. He was the kind of man who made her suspicious, but grudgingly she had to admit that he was attractive.

'Do I know you?' she asked, politely but coolly.

He held out his hand. 'Not yet. My name's Mike Donovan, I'm the new obs and gynae senior registrar. Apparently part of my job once a week is to lecture some of your students. I was hoping we might have a couple of words about the work. I'm a bit lost.'

Well, if it was work, Jenny was very happy to talk to the man. She took the proffered hand. 'Jenny Carson, Dr Donovan. I'm looking forward to working with you.'

And, in fact, she thought she was. This man had a presence, a good voice. If he knew his stuff, he'd be a good lecturer. And if John Bennet had appointed him, he would know his stuff.

'Call me Mike. You're Jenny. Look, if you don't have to rush off, could we sit somewhere and you could tell me what's involved? I've been in South America for the past five years. I've done a fair amount of training midwives there, but many of them couldn't speak English and much of our equipment was a bit rudimentary. This is going to be different.'

It seemed a reasonable request to make. But this was really a party and he was a good-looking man. Not a good combination. And she wondered about the polite but undeniably admiring way he was looking at her. Still… 'I think I can stay for a few more minutes,' she said. Then she wondered why she had said it. She should have gone straight home.

She had to admit that he got things done. Within moments of her accepting he had escorted her back to the party room, had found a table for two in a secluded corner and had somehow obtained a bottle of wine and two glasses.

'Just one glass, I'm driving,' she said. 'Now, what do you want to know?'

'Tell me what academic standard the students start at, what kind of tests they've taken before you offer them a place.'

He was certainly efficient. His questions were good. After fifteen minutes he knew exactly what was needed of him, exactly how he had to deliver it. And that pleased Jenny, he'd be a worthwhile colleague. 'I'm a lot clearer and happier now,' he said. 'I'm glad we've had this talk. Now I know what to do when faced with a group of eager young students demanding knowledge. Work over, Jenny. Now, would you like to dance? I'd love to dance with you.'

It came as a surprise. She had been so immersed in talking about work that she'd almost forgotten they were technically at a party. 'No,' she said, almost automatically. Then she looked at the swaying bright dresses on the dance floor, the ripple of lights. It did look fun. And she realised she'd been rather rude. 'I don't dance much,' she said.

'It's easy. In South America dancing is a way of life. I used to love it. Sure you won't try?'

He was persuasive but gentle, she liked that. And one dance wouldn't hurt. And they were going to work together. So she danced with him, and in moments was transported to a different world.

She had told him she didn't dance much, and that was true of the past three years. But before that she had never been happier than on a dance floor. And Mike took her back to those times, he was so good! At first he led her carefully, she found it easy to anticipate what he was going to do next. Soon she found herself slipping into old habits. She gave herself to the music, moving her body with a lack of restraint that caused surprised looks from the other dancers.

There was a long chord from the group on the dais. 'And now,' the leader shouted, 'Latin America time? Let's samba!'

Jenny made to walk from the floor. 'Don't think I can do this,' she said.

He held her back. 'But I can and I can show you. The samba is a dance for carnival. At carnival time everyone wears something new—even the poorest girl can afford something, even if it's only a brightly coloured scarf. This crowd looks like a carnival crowd. Look at the colours!'

'I don't look bright,' she said.

'Then you must show people that you feel bright. By dancing. Come on, you can sense the rhythm, just follow my steps. I know you can do that.'

So she did. And after a couple of minutes she was transported again, to a land of music and brightly coloured scarves.

The music stopped. To her amazement she and Mike were clapped by the others on the floor. She blushed. 'My students are amazed that the old woman can dance at all,' she said.

'You're not old. Don't ever put yourself down. And your students clapped because they were happy for you and knew you were happy. Now, shall we—?'

But she knew it was time for her to go. She had acted out of character for too long, she had to revert to the old, serious, distant Jenny Carson. 'I think I'd better go home now,' she said. 'It's been nice meeting you, Dr Donovan—Mike—but I have things to do.'

'If you really must, of course. I'll walk you to your car.'

She was glad that he didn't try to insist that she stay, and so she didn't object when he walked to her car with her.

It was interesting to observe him as they walked out of the club. He took a deep breath, stretched back his shoulders, thrust his arms out to the side. The simple physical act of walking seemed to give him pleasure. He seemed a man who enjoyed moving, who was happy in his body. Not like— Don't think that way!

'It's still quite early,' he said as they crossed to the car park. 'I don't suppose I could take you out to dinner?'

'It's kind of you to ask, but no. I have refused one invitation already—and, really, I try to keep my professional life and my personal life apart.'

'I see. A general principle or because of something that happened in the past?'

He was too bright! He had no right to ask that! And he must have seen the momentary look of pain on her face because he quickly said, 'Sorry. Asking impertinent questions is a nasty habit of mine. I'm trying to stop.'

They walked to her car in still companionable silence and as she unlocked the door he said, 'You know, I've not bought a car yet. You could drop me off somewhere.'

She grinned. 'Mike, I'm not a fool. I've met men who wanted to be dropped off before. Why don't you go back to the party and dance? There's lots of nurses there who are dying to meet a man like you. But I've enjoyed talking to you. Goodnight.'

She held out a hand for him to shake. He took the hand, quickly lifted it and kissed it. He said, 'I won't go back. There won't be another woman there like you.' He said it smilingly, almost as a joke. Then, before she realised what was happening, he leaned forward and swiftly kissed her lips. 'Stolen kisses are sweetest,' he said. 'Goodnight, Jenny.'

He stood back as she slammed her car door and started the engine. Then he raised his hand as the car moved away.

Jenny couldn't get her mixed thoughts in order. She ought to be angry with him. Why wasn't she? He'd kissed her. She hadn't been kissed like that by a man in over three years. Why had she let him kiss her? She had to be brutally honest with herself. She hadn't really objected.

She could like him as a colleague. She suspected he'd be very competent, very hard-working. But he had this casual air, as if life were a bit of a joke. And Jenny knew very well that life was hard.

She just couldn't be attracted to him. She was

Jenny Carson, everyone knew she wasn't interested in men. But she had quite enjoyed the dancing.

Mike watched the disappearing taillights and took a deep breath. Perhaps he shouldn't have kissed her. For a moment there the old Mike Donovan had come out, the Mike who would take a chance, go for what he wanted at once and dismiss the consequences.

Not a good idea right now. He wanted so desperately to get to know Jenny Carson—he should have been more cautious, taken his time. One stolen kiss might have ruined any chance of them getting closer. And made it hard for them to work together.

But perhaps not. When he had kissed her he had first seen panic flare in her eyes. But then there had been something else. An acceptance perhaps—even if a grudging one?

Perhaps it hadn't been too bad an idea. Perhaps this was some kind of a beginning.

Saturday morning, Mike felt that life was good.

He sat in the kitchen of his sister Sue's house, wearing, as ordered, an apron. On his knee was his nephew, three-year-old Sam. Known as Slippery Sam, Sam could wriggle out of anyone's grasp. But for the moment he was happy to sit on Uncle Mike's knee and eat enormous amounts of cereal. Sue was boiling breakfast eggs.

'I know you tend to fall in love every five minutes,' Sue said. 'Practically every letter you sent home had details of a different girl. But this is a bit quick even for you.'

'I didn't fall in love with them,' Mike protested. 'I just enjoyed their company. I made it clear that I was passing through, that whatever there was between us had to be short.'

'Yes. I've heard that before, it's every man's excuse. Now, what about this girl you met yesterday?'

He trusted his sister as much as anyone he knew, but for the moment he wasn't going to tell her exactly how he felt. For a start, it was all a shock to him, too. 'Well, I'm not in love with her either. Not yet. I just found her very attractive and very good to talk to. You say you don't know her?'

'It is one of the largest hospitals in Europe. I work part time in A and E, apparently she works in Obs and Gynae. Of course I don't know her.'

'Well, do you know anyone in Obs and Gynae? Anyone you could phone?'

Sue sighed. 'I've got a friend there. I suppose I could phone and ask if she knows anything. But I'm not promising anything.'

'Great. I could always rely on my big sister to keep me out of trouble. You say you want to go to the town market today?'

'Yes. You can either take Sam to the park or the pair of you can come with me.'

'Train!' shouted Sam through a mouthful of cereal. 'Uncle Mike's taking me on the train in the market.'

'Looks like town,' said Mike. 'You shop, we'll have an ice cream each. And Sam can go on the yellow train.'

\* \* \*

Jenny was in an odd mood. She had come to the town centre to go shopping, but there didn't seem to be much that she wanted. Perhaps she just needed to keep moving. Now she was in the indoor market, vaguely looking at a clothes shop.

When she was working as a college lecturer she could wear uniform or not. She chose a sister's uniform. And a sister's uniform when she was on the wards. Since she didn't have much of a social life, she tended most of the rest of her time to dress in shirt and jeans. So she didn't have much need for any fancy clothes.

Now she had stopped at a small shop that sold nothing but belts and scarves. A vast, colourful collection of silk scarves.

She didn't need a silk scarf. For winter she had a couple of woollen scarves that did her quite well, why should she need a silk scarf? And then she had to own up to herself that it was because of what Mike had told her the previous night, about even the poorest girl being able to afford a bright silk scarf for carnival. Well, there was to be no carnival in her life. But she could afford a silk scarf.

It took a satisfying twenty minutes in front of a large mirror to decide on the scarf that suited her best. At first she tried the more restrained colours, whites and greys or pastel shades. But then she thought carnival—and held the brilliant crimsons, the brightest of yellows against her hair. Eventually she bought a scarf that had a pattern of peacocks, with a deep, dark red border. That was bright enough for anyone. And it was packed in a shiny carrier bag, coloured purple. She wasn't quite sure when she might wear the scarf. But she was glad she had bought it.

As she wandered through the market, she wondered about her flat. Perhaps it was time she considered some decorating. It was clean, tidy enough—but it was hardly striking. For the past three years she had been frantically coping with her lecturing job. Work had been everything to her. Was now the time to think a bit about herself?

For no special reason whatsoever, she felt happy. Life could get better.

The market was on more than one level. At the centre was a concourse with escalators winding down from floor to floor. On the ground floor there was an open-air café and a small fair for the youngest children. Jenny took the escalator, started to descend. There were more shops below.

Then suddenly, very close, she saw him. Mike. He looked good, dressed casually in dark jeans and a white polo shirt. Jenny blinked. He was holding a small boy with obvious affection. And as she watched, a pretty blonde woman walked towards the pair, smiling and holding up her parcels. Mike kissed her. He kissed the woman. He had kissed *her* last night.

Jenny stiffened with dismay—more than dismay, with disappointment—and anger. She hadn't asked him if he was married, if he had a family. Why should she? But he could have said. And now the escalator was nearly at the bottom and she would have to get off and pass right by him.

He saw her, looked surprised then smiled. 'Jenny! What are you—?'

His lack of shame made things worse. She gave him a perfunctory nod, pushed past him and ran to the up escalator. And she stared straight ahead. No way did she want to look again at the happy domestic scene she had just witnessed. No way did she want to speak to Dr Mike Donovan.

So she was even more horrified when she stepped off the escalator to find him right behind her. He must have handed over the child then chased after her. And he wasn't even out of breath.

'Jenny, I—'

'Sorry, I'm in a hurry. I've got no time to stop and chat.'

She tried to move on but he took her arm, moved smartly to stand in front of her. Quickly he said, 'Jenny, I'd like you to come down and meet my sister and my nephew Sam. We're about to have an ice cream—would you like to join us?'

Sister? Jenny felt confused—then blushed an unbecoming red as she realised he had guessed what she been thinking. Then she became angry—at herself. 'I still have no time,' she said.

'We're going to work together so you'll be bound to meet them some time. They're part of my life. You may as well meet them now. Please, come and have an ice cream.'

Then he noticed the bright purple bag. 'You've been shopping. May I see what you've bought?'

She couldn't resist, her anger evaporated. 'I suppose I've time for an ice cream,' she said. 'And I bought a scarf. Listening to you last night made me do it. And I'm sorry I rushed past you just now but I—'

'Forget it. Just decide what ice cream, what sauce, what sprinklings you want on it.'

So she went down the escalator again. 'This is my sister Sue, who has looked after me all my life,' Mike introduced them. 'And this is Slippery Sam, my nephew.'

'Want ice cream now,' Sam said, 'with red stuff on.'

'Well, I'll take orders and then you can come with me. At least you know what you want.' Jenny found herself sitting chatting to the woman who was the sister of the man she…well, she guessed she liked. Certainly the only man she had met in the past three years who could— Jenny shied away from the thought.

'You must excuse my little brother,' said Sue, 'Well, all six feet two of him. I'd half forgotten what he was like, but it's good to have him back. And Harry's pleased he's staying with us. Says it'll make sure the lawn gets mowed.'

'Who's Harry?'

'My husband. He's another doctor, but at the moment he's away with the army abroad. He's in the reserves.' She went on. 'He'll be back soon and I've got a surprise for him.'

There was a glint in Sue's eyes and Jenny realised that she recognised it. 'A brother or a sister for Sam?'

Sue nodded. 'I gather you work in Obs and Gynae so you're going to see more of me.'

'That'll be nice. How do you know I work in Obs and Gynae?'

'Mike told me about you this morning. At some length. You'll have to get used to him. If he's enthusiastic about anything, everyone knows about it.'

Jenny pondered a moment. How and why should Mike be enthusiastic about her? But she decided to not press the question. Instead, she asked, 'Does Mike know about your new arrival?'

'It's magic. I don't know how he does it. He came into the house, dropped his bags, looked at me and said, "When is it due?"'

Mike came back, carrying a tray. 'Ice creams for the two most important women in my life.'

'I can't be important to you,' Jenny pointed out. 'You only met me yesterday.'

'You're going to be my boss when I lecture. I'm terrified.' He sat down, carefully gave out the ice creams and then negotiated with Sam for a small share of his red sauce.

'And I gather you're going to be an uncle again?'

'I'm looking forward to it. I like kids.'

'Why don't you have some of your own, then?' Sue demanded.

He looked mournful. 'No woman will have me. Well, not the ones I really fancy.'

'Your trouble is, you're too picky,' said Jenny. She was enjoying herself more than she had done for quite a while. She had forgotten what fun it could be to have a good, daft conversation.

'That's me, picky. All I want is the best. Like my brother-in-law Harry. He got the best. He got Sue.'

Sue patted his hand. 'Your charm isn't working, Mike. You still have to weed the garden this afternoon.'

He sighed. 'Somewhere out there, I know there's the perfect woman for me. I just know it. All I have to do is to find her. Are you a perfect woman, Jenny?'

It was said in the same joking tone, but in his eyes she thought she saw the flash of a deeper meaning. This was more than a joke.

She took a spoonful of ice cream while she thought of an answer. Only Mike was listening. Sue was trying to wipe Sam's face. 'I'm pretty perfect at my job,' she said after a while, using the same light-hearted tone, 'but I'm not the perfect woman for you, or anyone else.'

'I'll need convincing,' said Mike.

They parted soon after that. Sam had to get home for his dinner. Sue asked her to come round for supper one night. 'Wait till you've worked with Mike for a while. See if you can stand seeing more of him. And he'll cook. He came home from abroad an expert in all sorts of dishes.'

'You must try my chicken in chocolate,' said Mike.

'Chicken in chocolate? Honestly?'

'Don't think of that milky sugary brown stuff you buy in bars. The real chocolate. I think you'll be surprised.'

'I'd like to try it,' Jenny said, but feeling doubtful.

'See you on Monday,' Mike went on. 'I'll be the one in the white coat, feeling lost and tearful.'

'I'll look out for you. Make sure you have your name sewn into your coat.'

She felt a bit lost herself when they had gone, and went and bought herself a coffee. They seemed a happy, close family. Something she had never really been a part of. She wondered what Harry, the husband, was like. She was willing to bet that he was nice, too. Sue had good taste.

She left the market shortly afterwards and went to the nearest big store. Outside she looked at the scarf she had bought. It was a scarf to go with a dress. Usually, she only bought dresses when she needed them—which wasn't very often. She hadn't needed a party dress in—that time span again—three years. Well, so what?

She searched through three stores, then she bought herself a green dress that matched her eyes and went well with the scarf. She thought she'd had a good morning.

# CHAPTER TWO

HOME was a small top-floor flat in a modern block
to the north of the city. Jenny had bought it because
if you stood on a stool there was a view of the sea,
and because she felt alone and isolated up here.
Which was what she wanted. This was her kingdom,
her kingdom only.

First she had to try on her new dress. When she
did she knew she looked good in it. With the right
shoes, make-up and hairstyle she'd look better than
just good. All she had to do now was find an occasion to wear it. The thought intrigued her. Recently
she hadn't been interested in going out. She took off
the dress, put on her jeans again and wandered
around the flat.

It was comfortable but it wasn't exciting. She had
persuaded herself that she hadn't had time for other
things, her job alone concerned her. There had been
a lot to set up and run. But now the job was running
smoothly, she knew she could afford to relax a little.
Think of herself.

As Jenny wandered she decided that the rooms
perhaps needed another coat of paint, a bit more furniture. She could do with a new carpet in the living
room. She opened the built-in wardrobe in her bedroom, it was nowhere near full. And the clothes there
were largely functional. Suits for work, a selection

of casual gear for hanging around the flat. Apart from today, she could hardly remember the last time she had shopped for something colourful and bright.

She looked in what should be the second bedroom—now converted into her office. Then she surveyed the expensive computer, the steel shelves full of files, the boxes of notes, carefully in order. It looked coldly efficient—not homely. Not even one picture on the wall!

Feeling more distracted than ever, she made herself a coffee, threw herself down onto her couch. When had she last had a proper holiday? Not for years! She'd been on courses trying to improve her skills.

The thought came—unwelcome. She needed a life!

Why was she feeling this way, dissatisfied with everything around her? She didn't have to look far for the answer. It was obviously Dr Mike Donovan. She had only met him twice but he seemed to have had an enormous effect on her. She wouldn't have thought he was her sort of man. She was cautious, he was a risk-taker. She always thought first, he acted on impulse.

She frowned. What kind of doctor was he? But she wasn't worried. Something told her that he'd never take a risk with a patient, never cut corners. She didn't know why, she just knew it. Perhaps it was the careful, loving way she had seen him handling his nephew.

But this dissatisfaction wasn't Mike's fault, it was hers. She knew she was attractive, had the normal female urges. Three years ago she had coolly decided to cut herself off from male company. There had been plenty of offers since but she had turned them all down.

Perhaps she was ready for a change? But she was afraid. It would be easier to stay as she was.

Sunday was hot. Mike rose early, mowed the lawn and then dug over the vegetable patch, weeded the flower-beds and trimmed the hedges. For an hour he helped Sam with his little garden. Then, hot, sweaty and dirty, he went inside for a shower. It was now evening. He sat outside on the patio with Sue, ate salad and drank a glass of wine.

'You've always been the same when you're thinking,' Sue said. 'It's easier for you to think if you're working hard. What's worrying you?'

He shrugged. 'Nothing's worrying me. I'm looking forward to starting work.'

'Of course you are.' Sue sipped her wine. 'I liked Jenny Carson, liked her a lot. But you've only met her twice. Is she the one you're wondering about? Remember when you were younger, you used to ask me my opinion about girls?'

'I'm older now,' he said.

'So am I. And perhaps I'm a bit more careful. This morning, while you were slaving away, I phoned my friend in Obs and Gynae. She knows Jenny. Mike, you are not to mess around with her! She's been hurt enough.'

Mike stared down the garden, looked at a black-bird industriously picking over the ground he had dug. 'I've been home a month now. I haven't met anyone who has impressed me as she has. In fact, I haven't met anyone like her in years. Hurting her is the last thing I want to do.'

'Hmm. Little brother lady-killer seems to have grown up at last. Well, I'll tell you what I learned. Nothing secret, you'll find it out yourself in the next few days. Jenny is an ice maiden. She's just not interested in men, but no one knows why. Pity really, she's an attractive woman. The students love her because she's fair and a good teacher and gets them through their exams. She turns out first-rate midwives. And she's tough. She'll stand no nonsense from her patients and is reputed to have thrown a drunken husband out of the ward when he didn't want to go. Threw him out almost physically.'

'She enjoyed confronting him?'

'Well, she didn't back away. She backs away from no one. She expects respect from the senior medical staff and she gets it. When she's in charge things are run properly.'

'She sounds like a challenge.'

'Mike, she is not a challenge! No one knows why she is anti-men. She came here from a London hospital three years ago and that's all anyone knows about her. She's a loner. She's everyone's friend and no one's close friend.'

'I see,' said Mike.

'So what are you going to do about her?'

'I want to see more of her. If she's an ice maiden I want to know if she'll melt.'

'You be careful,' Sue warned him. 'I've only met her once but I like her. Cause her trouble and you'll answer to me.'

This was Jenny's world, here she felt at home. The lecture theatre was full of cheerful chattering trainee midwives. Jenny knew them all, had taught them for a couple of years now.

She stood on the dais in front of the class, sorted through the papers she had to deal with. Then she looked up and smiled. 'Good morning, everyone!'

A chorus of greetings came back. Then there was silence. Jenny had made it clear very quickly that when she talked, no one else did.

There were a couple of announcements about the week's programme and then Jenny realised one person was missing. 'Where's Ann Mallon?'

Silence from the class. There were some uncomfortable stirrings and then one nurse said hesitantly, 'I think she's got stomach cramps.'

Jenny nodded, as if this was all right. 'I'll drop in to see her,' she said, knowing that Ann Mallon was taking too much time off. Her written work was poor, her practical work only just satisfactory. Jenny would try to find out the reason, help Ann if she could. If she was just malingering then perhaps a career other than midwifery would suit her better. But that was for later. More pleasant things first.

'We have a new lecturer today,' Jenny said. 'Dr Donovan. He's the new senior registrar on Obs and Gynae. You'll be seeing a lot of him when you do your practical work. I'll leave him to introduce himself.'

She nodded to the door Mike had been waiting outside, watching her through the glass panel. He came in at once.

Even his walk was full of energy, Jenny thought. He strode across the room, jumped rather than stepped onto the dais.

Jenny could feel a flutter of interest among the midwives. She smiled rather sourly to herself. The interest wasn't because of the lecture—but because of the lecturer. And when they saw the scar, the interest deepened. Mike looked good. Rather a contrast from the previous lecturer, Dr Relph, who was highly competent but tubby, bespectacled and balding.

'A very good morning to you all. My name is Dr Mike Donovan. I've come to talk about the respective parts played by midwives and doctors. Before I start, I want to emphasise that I believe both parts are equally important. And in the delivery suite the midwife rules.'

That was a good start, Jenny thought. He's got their interest and respect.

'I think you're entitled to know a bit about me so that when we talk you'll know I know what I'm talking about. For the past five years I've worked for a large charity in a variety of countries in South America. I've helped to train a lot of midwives. And I learned there that a set of trained midwives could do far more good than a single doctor. Midwifery must be one of the most satisfying branches of medicine. Now, when you first hear that…'

Jenny stayed for his lecture. She was entitled to as technically in this department she was Mike's boss.

And he was good. He knew his material, even better he knew how to feed it in a little at a time, how to emphasise the important points. She wouldn't need to sit in on his lectures again, she knew he was more than competent. But perhaps she would...

It had been strange, meeting him on Saturday morning. But she felt more in control here, in her own set of rooms, dressed in her uniform. And she knew he had sensed that she wanted their relationship to be purely professional. At least for an hour or two and in this place. They would have to get used to working together. But the more she saw of him, the more she was...attracted to him? It might have been easier for her if he'd been a poor lecturer. But he was good—very good.

His lecture was finishing. The time seemed to have passed very quickly. 'Now, questions. And I want to say that at any time you are working with me, you can ask questions. It's the best way to learn. I may not be able to answer at once—but I'll find time.'

And there were questions—more than usual.

But finally the class was dismissed. A couple of the nurses stopped him in the corridor. Well, serve him right for making the offer about questions. Jenny drifted past, listening. They were good questions. The girls wanted to learn, not just chat to a handsome new lecturer. And Mike was having fun answering the questions.

Then someone new came down the corridor. A portly, self-important-looking man in a shiny blue suit, clutching a sheaf of papers. He barged straight into Mike's conversation, interrupting him. 'Dr

Donovan, I'm Mr Kaye, from Human Resources. I have these forms for you. I want to process them at once. Could you see to them now?'

Jenny saw Mike look at the man, and she didn't like the expression on Mike's face. But he merely held out his hand and said, 'Leave them with me. I'll do them when I can.'

Mr Kaye shook his head. 'I really need them now. I'm sure you have time and we're very busy in our office. You can deal with these…students later.' There was dislike in the word 'students'.

Mike looked at Mr Kaye. A hand went up and caressed the scar on his cheek. Jenny stared at the two and even though she was hardened she shivered at the expression on Mike's face. He turned to the two trainee midwives and said, very pleasantly, 'Would you excuse me for exactly thirty seconds?' Then he turned to Mr Kaye, took him by the arm and marched him down the corridor.

Jenny saw them coming, stepped inside a classroom door. She left it partly open so she could, quite unashamedly, listen.

Mike's voice was a snarled whisper. Jenny had only ever heard him be pleasant so it came as a shock. 'Listen, you little jobsworth. Our job here is healing the sick and training others how to do it. Everything else comes second to that. Filling in forms comes bottom of my priorities. Now, I will fill these in, when I have time and when I have finished the important part of my work. But for now, go away and file some paperclips and don't bother me!'

Two sets of footsteps. Mr Kaye set off rapidly. Mike went back to talk to the two nurses. Jenny wondered.

'How did I do, miss? Did I pass my practical?' Mike sat in Jenny's office, completely at ease.

'You passed your teaching assessment. Definitely. I hope you don't come to regret the offer you made about answering questions.'

'I won't. I meant every word. Asking questions is the best way of learning. I'm glad you're pleased.'

'I'm not so pleased about the next bit, with the man from Human Resources. Just which school of charm did you go to? That clerk was only doing his job. Why pick on him?'

Imperturbably, Mike glanced at the sheaf of papers in his hand. 'Doing his job? He was enjoying it too much. He didn't realise the importance of what those girls were doing, he was a paper-pushing bully. And, most important, I've already filled in those forms once—in triplicate, as required. He's lost them. Sister Carson, excessive paperwork in hospitals has caused more trouble than most of the viruses I know.'

She sighed. She had to agree with him. Paperwork was the bane of her life. But she'd never thought to challenge any of the Mr Kayes around her. They seemed to work to their own set of rules.

'It's lunchtime,' Mike went on. 'Would you like to come over to the hospital canteen with me? I'll buy you an egg sandwich.'

She shook her head. 'I bring my own sandwiches with me. I sit here and work, and drink lots of coffee.'

'Ah, dedication. If I go out and buy my own sandwich, will you let me work in your office? I think I
need to access some of your files. And perhaps you
might spare me a coffee, too?'

'All right. But I'm not going to spend the time
chatting. I do have work to do.'

'Perfect. I'll fetch my sandwich. Back in ten
minutes.'

She made the coffee while he was gone, found a
spare mug and then sat thinking about him. So far
today he had acted like the complete professional.
Their two previous meetings had been acknowl-
edged, but that was all. Jenny found that a bit disturbing. She wasn't sure what she did want from
Mike. She suspected it was a little more than this
bland acceptance of her. And he wanted to work in
her office.

He returned with his sandwich, she poured him a
coffee and showed him where her files were. Then
they both settled down to work. Both worked in
silence, apart from the occasional rustle of papers.

Her job was important. She had to write assessments of all her students. Later on these assessments
would be shown to the students and discussed. It was
a vital part of her work, she had to get it right. But
just now it was hard to concentrate.

And after a while she found his very silence irri-
tating. She glanced at him, he was absorbed in his
work.

He was a handsome man, she thought, lean and
muscular. A bit older than her, not much. Every time
she saw him she thought he was dressed well,

dressed correctly for the occasion. She liked his voice. She wondered what it would be like if he… Don't think that way! He was just a doctor in her room.

Eventually she could stand the silence no longer. Her voice was snappy as she said, 'You could have worked somewhere else, you know—why my room? You don't need to be here, there are other places far more comfortable. And don't say that you need to refer to my files. So far you've only looked at the one. You could have borrowed it.'

Why did she sound so irritated?

He swung round on his stool. He didn't seem either annoyed or amused. Instead, he looked pensive. He looked at her and after a while said, 'I wanted to be in the same room as you.'

'Why? In case you needed to ask me questions about the course?'

He took a while to answer. Then he pointed to a little mirror, it was one out of her handbag, she had left it flat on the bench. Now it was propped against the back wall. 'Every now and again I look at you in that mirror. It pleases me, you have a lovely face. And you have an aura. When I'm near you I can feel you, feel your warmth.'

She was bewildered. 'What are you talking about? I'm not a warm person, everyone knows I'm supposed to be cool. And this is only the third time we've met. How can you want to be near me?'

'Only the third time we've met? But I can remember every second of those times. And did you know, at the party, just how long I spent looking at you?

Before I'd even spoken to you? Jenny, I've never met anyone like you before.'

'This is silly! You can't just…just…form an attraction like that! It takes time. And anyway, what about me? I'm…I'm not sure I…' She didn't know what to say.

He stood, came over to her, picked up her hands in his. It was the lightest of grips, but she felt she couldn't make him let go. 'What about you, Jenny? The three times we've met, haven't you felt something between us? Jenny, try to be honest—to me and to yourself.'

It was a challenge. She made a supreme effort, managed to draw her hands from his. 'I don't think about men much at all,' she said. 'I'm happy as I am. I made that decision a while ago.'

'I'm not men. I'm me, an individual. Someone you've just met. And decisions can be altered.'

Her voice was almost a wail. 'But I don't want to change. I told you, I'm happy the way I am. I can do without the heartache.'

'Heartache. Interesting word. Tell me why you used it.'

'No.'

A single short word, but he accepted it in its certainty.

He seemed to be thinking, and Jenny didn't know quite what to do, think or say. Not ten minutes before she had been reasonably content in her life. Now this man had thrown that contentment into question.

'We'll be working together much of this week,' he said after a while. 'I've got a couple more lectures to give and I gather I'm going to be seeing you on the antenatal ward. So far I've got next Saturday off. How about you?'

'I get most weekends off. Unless I volunteer for an awkward shift, a Saturday night or something. I often do that. But I'm off this weekend. Why?' She wondered if she ought to ask. 'I hope you're not going to ask me out. Because the answer will be no.'

'Are you afraid of me or afraid of yourself?'

It was a question she didn't want to answer. She kept silent.

After a while he said, 'I need exercise. Real exercise, not pushing machines in a gym. I need to walk.' He smiled at her—it was such an infectious smile! 'In this hospital I just walk into a ward. A lot of my time recently I've had to climb two or three thousand feet before I can reach a clinic. And I miss it! You've got walking boots, haven't you? And I'll bet you haven't used them for a while.'

The two questions threw her. 'Well, yes, I have got boots, and it is a while since I went on a long walk. I…used to walk a lot. Not recently, though. But I told you, I don't go out with men. And I don't mix business with pleasure.'

He went on as if he hadn't heard her. 'I want to walk out of the Conway valley, up and round a lake in the hills. You won't be walking with a man, just a person. A friend even. Think of it like that. I suspect you'll love it.'

When she thought about it, the idea of a walk in Snowdonia was attractive. And he was right, she hadn't been out for quite a time. Not even a proper holiday for three years…

'How would we get to the Conway valley?' she asked, knowing she was weakening.

He shrugged. 'I'll hire a car. I'm going to buy myself a new one soon, I just haven't got round to it.'

'If we go, we can take my car. Or are you too proud to be driven by a woman?'

She wondered if he knew this was a test.

If it was a test, he passed it. He laughed. 'In Peru I had the experience of a woman older than me carrying my rucksack because the altitude was too high and I just couldn't breathe. I'm not proud. We'll decide on details later. So, you will come?'

She wasn't even sure herself why she said yes. Perhaps it was because she quite liked Mike, perhaps it was because she'd realised that her life recently had been rather dreary and she deserved a change. And a walk in the hills sounded good. But… 'Mike! This is just two friends going for a walk together. Nothing more.'

'Whatever else?' he asked.

Straight afterwards Mike said that he'd got the facts he needed from her files, there were a couple of things that he'd better check with the consultant. Once in the corridor he let out a great sigh of relief, took out his handkerchief and ran it over his hair. That meeting had been close! He'd tried to appear calm. But if only she knew just how tense he had been!

Still, she'd agreed to spend a day with him. That was a success.

It had been a deliberate decision on his part. Either he could stay as an amiable colleague of Jenny's and try to interest her little by little, or he could try shock tactics. He'd decided on the second. It was a natural thing for him to do. And he didn't want her to see him as just another man she had to work with.

He still wondered why she'd agreed to go with him. Perhaps at long last the ice maiden was thawing out. And as for two friends just going on a walk…well, they would see.

And he still thought she was the most gorgeous thing he had seen in years.

As ever, at home that evening Jenny was working on her computer. She had finished the six-monthly assessments of her students and was checking them against previous assessments to see if there were any problems that needed to be addressed. Apart from the situation with Ann Mallon, which was being monitored, there were none.

She hadn't needed to work. It was displacement activity. Just a way of avoiding thinking about something that was troubling her. Thinking about Mike. How had he persuaded her into going out for the day with him? She didn't go out with men. How had he got her to change her mind?

Her thoughts wouldn't go away so finally she closed the students' files and gazed sightlessly at her screensaver. Silver birds flying over blue seas did nothing for her. What should she do about Mike?

Had it started with that first kiss—only three nights before?

Her thoughts were in a turmoil. Then she remembered a technique she had learned, of all people, from her Guide leader many years before. Problems became simpler if you wrote them down.

On her computer Jenny created a spreadsheet—the oddest use of a spreadsheet format she could remember. As the title she typed 'Jenny Carson—Love Life'. There were five columns. Mike's name, his age, her age, for, against. Then, with a giggle, she started to fill in the columns.

When the columns were nearly finished, she looked over what she had got down.

First real boyfriend ever, Jack Mayhew. He had been seventeen, she had been fifteen. For—well, at that age you just had to have a boyfriend. Everyone had one. And Jack had been both good-looking and older, she had been proud to be seen out with him. Besides, he'd helped her with her science homework. Against? Well, the usual male thing. He'd wanted more than she'd been prepared to give. But she had loved kissing him. The thought flashed through her mind— How long had it been since she had enjoyed being kissed that way? Mike had kissed her. But only quickly.

Jenny shook her head. She had parted more or less friends with Jack. In fact, she had lost him to an older, more experienced girl. Lisa Quist had been nineteen—even older than Jack. And it had been said that Linda was willing to…well, that was years ago.

On to the next one. When training as a nurse, a

young doctor, Martin Meres. An earnest, eager, nervous young man. For—they'd got on well, had shared interests. But there had been no real passion there. When he'd found a post at a distant hospital they'd written to each other. But only for a while.

Next, Lennie Rossiter. He had been a junior registrar and with him for the first time she'd felt the power of real emotions. What he'd felt for her had both thrilled and frightened her. For—she had been sure that she loved him, physically at least. Against—she hadn't been sure that she'd liked him. One night he'd taken her for granted, they'd argued and after that she'd dropped him.

He'd tried to get her back but she wouldn't have him. He had been really angry with her—and had taken his revenge by telling stories about her. She'd hated that.

Interesting. Whatever happened, she was certain that Mike would never do anything like that. Why was she so certain?

There were a couple more men. One was a hospital manager, one was from the outside world—a solicitor. She had very much liked them both, but she hadn't felt that passion for them that she felt she was ultimately capable of.

Then she'd met Peter Murphy. She'd thought—she'd known—that this had been the man who could give her everything she needed.

She printed his name on the paper. Then she looked through the rest of the list and deleted every name. All the rest were irrelevant. Peter was the biggest thing—the only thing—in her emotional life. He would take a lot of getting over—if indeed she ever did get over him.

When she thought of him, she shivered. And she promised herself that, whatever else happened, she would not let Mike Donovan get too close to her.

In fact, she had to work with Mike the next day when he was conducting his rounds on the antenatal ward. Jenny had arranged for four of her midwifery students to shadow the doctor, the SHO and the ward manager as they checked on all the patients and decided on the future pattern of care.

'They're new, this is their first time in hospital,' she said to Mike. 'If they can just observe, afterwards I'll answer any questions they might have.'

'Like I said in my lecture, I'll happily answer questions. Just so long as they're asked at the appropriate time.'

'No one will say a word to you in front of a patient. They have been told that several times. But if you want to talk to them as you're walking, great.'

Jenny didn't go on the ward round, it was busy enough already. She sat in the ward manager's room and looked through the patients' notes. It stopped her thinking about Mike.

Eventually the ward round was over. With the ward manager Jenny arranged for her four students to each shadow a nurse. This time they would be encouraged to speak to the patients, to try to provide some of the comfort and support that was so necessary to women who could be anxious. And afterwards Jenny would ask them what they had noticed, what questions they had.

She believed in the importance of time on the wards, and had a suspicion that the modern plan of a programme of initial lectures and classes was no substitute for practical time. But she didn't say this too loudly to her university colleagues.

Mike hadn't come back to the ward manager's office. Apparently he wanted to chat—informally he said—to one of the patients. Jenny wondered if he'd come and chat to her. Then she went on with her work.

Things altered quite a bit ten minutes later.

A nurse popped her head round the door and said, 'Jenny? If you feel like being a referee, you might like to go on the ward. I think our new Dr Donovan is going to kill one of the fathers.'

'Kill him? That's a bit extreme.' Jenny sighed. For some reason there often seemed to be an excess of trouble with fathers in the antenatal ward. Perhaps they were worried or stressed. Postnatal ward was much quieter. 'Which father?'

'Mr Brent. The doctor has taken him out of the ward into the rest room.'

Mr Brent. If something nasty happened to Mr Brent, Jenny wouldn't be too worried. When he came in he tended to be drunk—even in the afternoon. Or he'd been taking something even worse. And when Jenny had undressed his white-faced wife, she had found bruises that certainly did not come from 'falling against the furniture'.

But she wasn't sure that Mike was the right person to deal with Mr Brent.

She hurried down the ward to the little side room

that the nurse indicated. Mike was standing, his face black with anger, his arms folded, staring down at a smaller figure who was sitting uncomfortably in a low easy chair. As Jenny watched, Mr Brent tried to struggle to his feet. Mike put a hand on his shoulder, pressed him down again.

'I haven't finished with you yet,' he said. 'You may talk to people how you like in your own home, but you don't do it in my ward. Especially, you don't speak to your wife that way. She's about to go through a painful and disturbing process. She needs support. And more than that, you speak to my nurse politely. If she can't answer your questions she'll refer you to me. Now, do you understand me?'

'You can't speak to me like that! I'll report you.'

'I *can* speak to you like that, I just have done. In future, when you want to come on this ward you'll have to wait outside until we can arrange for a member of Security to come in with you. Get that?'

Jenny blinked at what happened next. Mike's hand dived into Brent's pocket, came out with a small packet of white powder. He looked at it, looked at Brent.

Jenny could see Mike's face. There was such an expression of hatred on it that for a moment she wondered if the nurse had been right and Mike was going to murder one of the fathers. And she saw the fear on Brent's face, too. Mike said nothing. She saw him struggle for control and eventually he seemed calmer. A bit calmer.

'I'm taking this,' he said. 'In fact, I'm stealing it.'

He pointed to a telephone. 'Why don't you phone the police and report me?'

The man's face twisted with fear and anger. 'You want to be careful. You might think that—'

Mike seized one of Brent's arms and hauled him upright. 'I've wasted enough time on you. Just go. And remember what I said about a security officer.' Then he frogmarched the man to the ward entrance and heaved him out.

Jenny watched him as he stood in the doorway, making sure that the man walked away. With one hand he was stroking the scar that ran down his cheek. She wondered if at times it pained him. But there were other things to consider.

'Was that entirely wise?' she asked him when he returned. She felt that her heartbeat was just returning to normal. The scene she had just witnessed might have been necessary, but it had been ugly.

Mike shrugged. 'Was it wise? Possibly not. But it was satisfying.'

'What was in the white packet and how did you know it was there?'

'It was cocaine. He left his wife for a while and went to the toilet. He must have sniffed it there. When he came back he was hyperactive and abusive. And I noticed that when we were arguing he kept on feeling in that pocket as if there was something there that would give him strength.'

Jenny sighed. 'You know, sometimes it's necessary but it's never a good idea to argue with fathers if you can help it. They tend to take out their anger on their wives. So what are we going to do about Mrs Brent?'

He looked at her. 'You already had your suspicions about that man, didn't you? I was talking to his wife, just casually, when he came in. And I saw the look in her eyes—fear. You'd have spotted that.'

'I was going to get in touch with Social Services,' said Jenny. 'Now we both can make a report. But we'll talk about that later.'

She thought for a minute. 'But now there's something else I want to talk to you about. At times we all get angry at patients and relations, and sometimes perhaps we're entitled to show how angry we are. But just then I thought you might be going a bit too far with that man. For a moment he was terrified of you.' She paused, and then said, honestly, 'In fact, I was a bit frightened of you myself.'

He looked dismayed. 'I didn't want that. Perhaps I overreacted but I'm afraid that casual drug use is something I feel a bit strongly about.'

But Jenny was thinking, something had just struck her. 'You've just come back from South America,' she said. 'Did you spend much time in Colombia?'

Now his expression was guarded. 'I spent some time there.'

'Colombia, where most of the world's cocaine comes from? The drug that you apparently know so much about and hate so much?'

'Yes, that Colombia,' he said.

Mike seemed to be getting agitated again. Jenny watched as he lifted his hand, stroked the scar on his cheek as he had done before. And Jenny made another wild guess. 'Is that where your cheek was slashed?'

And suddenly, mysteriously he was calm again. 'That's right.' He smiled. 'Clever of you to guess. No one in this country knows anything about it. I tend to keep it a secret. But if you want, I'll tell you.'

She did want to know. But she realised that if he told her, if they shared the intimacy of a secret, it would bring them closer together. Did she want that? Did she want to be closer to this man?

'I'd like you to tell me,' she said after a pause.

They sat together in the garden of the Setchell Arms, a pub and restaurant a couple of miles from the hospital. Mike had said that the story would take too long to tell in a busy ward, and they were bound to be interrupted if they sat together in her room. Besides, they were both busy.

So he'd asked her if she knew of anywhere pleasant where they could share a quiet drink after the day's work was done. She'd thought, suggested this place. It was far enough from the hospital for her to be reasonably certain that they wouldn't be seen by other hospital staff. 'Could we perhaps stay there for a meal?' he had asked.

She had refused. 'Sorry, got far too much work to do at home.' It was partly true.

So now they sat facing each other, he with a pint of beer, she with a glass of iced orange.

'You're touching your scar again,' she said to him as his hand strayed to his face. 'I've only seen you do that when you're angry or upset.'

'You're bright, Jenny. There's not a lot gets past you, is there? I've seen you with your students—do they know just how well you know them?'

She smiled briefly. 'I try to keep on top of what I'm doing. Knowing how my new midwives are going to react is an important part of my job. And knowing how the people who lecture for me are likely to react—I need to think about that, too.'

'I see. So you are here to have me explain why I'm so anti-drugs? Isn't nearly every doctor and nurse against them? Sue says that work in A and E could be halved if there were no addicts about.'

'Mike,' she said, 'you're avoiding the question. You came here to tell me something.'

He nodded. 'I'm trying to decide what to tell you, what's not really relevant.'

'Think of taking a medical history,' she said. 'Everything and anything may be relevant.'

'Very true. All right, I'll tell you everything. Some bits you might not like.'

She had to smile as his hand reached for his cheek again. He saw her smile, realised what he was doing and slammed his hand on the table. 'I'll cure myself of it,' he said.

'Have you thought about having plastic surgery? For that matter, why didn't you have it dealt with when you were first hurt?'

'Part of the story I'll tell you now.' He looked up, his eyes distant, and she guessed he wasn't seeing the lawns and shrubberies of the pub, but the forests of a distant country. And his voice altered, too, became reflective, as if he was reliving past events and wondering how they had occurred.

'About two years ago the charity I worked for asked—invited—me to work for six months in the highlands of Colombia. They wanted someone to run local clinics, perhaps give some basic training to people who wanted to become midwives. The only trouble was, they couldn't guarantee my safety. No one knew who controlled the area—government forces or the local guerrillas who grew and éxported the cocaine. But the charity thought that if I kept a low profile, if I was seen just to be helping the locals and their babies, I ought to be OK.'

'What about the local medical service?' Jenny asked. 'Weren't they competent?'

'The few who were left were competent, grossly overworked and had to manage with the minimum of equipment. I worked with them, got to like them.'

'Did you speak the language?'

'I could make myself understood—just. Not in the local native languages, of course, but I picked up enough to get by. And I was assigned a local translator who would also be my guide, drive me round, see that I got to work.'

His eyes lost their dreamy look as they focussed on Jenny. 'Her name was Inez Sanchez, she was three years younger than me and as beautiful as only those high-altitude women can be.' He paused. 'And I fell in love with her.'

'You did what?' Jenny looked at him, appalled. This wasn't the story she wanted to hear.

'I fell in love with her. I thought she was the

woman I'd spent my life looking for, the one I wanted to marry. But for the time being we had work to do. There were babies and mothers dying who didn't need to die. So they came first.'

'But did you…did the pair of you…?' Jenny couldn't decide how to ask.

'Did we sleep together? Yes.'

Jenny didn't know how she felt. He had fallen in love with a woman, had wanted to marry her, slept with her. Of course it was no concern of hers, she was entirely indifferent to his actions. Or was she? Why did she feel irritated at this confession—even feel that she had been let down?

'I thought you were going to tell me how your cheek got slashed,' she said. 'I didn't expect intimate details of your love life.'

Then she looked up to see him smiling at her, knew that he had guessed the cause of her irritation. And that made her more angry than ever.

'My love life and my cheek got mixed up,' he said.

Then she saw his face change, his previous mocking attitude disappear. She couldn't make out what he was feeling—angry, or bitter, or even sad. Once again he stroked the scar and this time she said nothing.

'I'd done a hard day's work and was lying in my room. I needed to rest. Then Inez came round, apparently very distressed. She said that she'd been visiting old family friends, and a young girl, the wife of one of the sons, had been in labour for twelve hours. There seemed to be complications, would I mind going to see her? It was a lot to ask, but they knew that if they brought her round to the local hospital it would be hours before she could be attended to. So I said I'd bring my medical kit and come along.'

'Go on,' Jenny said when he paused. The story was catching her interest. She could wonder or worry about Inez later.

'Inez drove me there. I was surprised at the distance from the town that we had to travel. I was also surprised at the direction, the area was suspected of being bandit country. Usually if we went that way we had an army escort. But Inez seemed confident enough.

'Then we came to this half-derelict farmhouse. We drove into the yard, and I was surprised when three alert young men came to check us, they all carried guns. But when they saw Inez, they relaxed. I was a bit put out, though. I asked Inez what was going on, she said not to worry, all would be revealed.

'We went into the farmhouse and saw more young men with guns. And we were taken to a bedroom to see my patient. But it wasn't a young girl in labour. It was a man with a bullet hole in his chest which had become infected. He was going to die. And when I held the light to his face, I recognised him, his face was on every second poster in the town. He was a guerrilla leader, controlled most of the cocaine-producing fields around for miles.'

By now Jenny couldn't hide her fascination. 'So there was no pregnant daughter-in-law?'

'No. I asked Inez what was happening, she said she'd explain. But I was a doctor, first I had to see to my patient. She knew enough medicine to realise that only urgent medical care would save him. And if he died I would pay for it. When I suggested that a hospital would be the best place for him, she laughed at me.'

'But you're not a surgeon!'

'I was that night. I was everything—anaesthetist, surgeon and scrub nurse. But I got the bullet out, cleaned up the wound, stitched him together and said that now at least he had a fighting chance. Could I, please, have an explanation and why had Inez betrayed me? I thought we were in love.'

Now he looked at Jenny directly. 'Ever been betrayed, Jenny? Do you know what it feels like? When you realise that everything you have counted on, believed in over the past few months has all been a sad farce.'

Suddenly Jenny felt a great sympathy for him. They had more in common than she had realised. 'I've been betrayed,' she said. 'Now finish your story.'

He shrugged. 'You can probably guess the rest. Inez was one of a family that had made millions out of the cocaine trade. In fact, the guerrilla leader was her cousin or something. She was quite interested in the work I was doing, believed that it helped the community. But, of course, family came first. And as for love...well, she quite liked me and it made her job more pleasant. Things could go on as they had been before. But there would be more cases like this. And I would be well paid.'

'So how did your face get slashed?'

He shrugged. 'I didn't tell Inez what I thought, I just said I needed some drugs from the car. A guard went with me as I went to look for them. I hit him, knocked him out and ran for the gate. Another guard came out, slashed at me with his machete—and caught me. They chased me but I kept running, and once I was in the dark and the forest, I managed to lose them. Though I was bleeding like no one's business.'

Jenny shivered at the horror of it. 'So…?'

'I found a track through the forest, ran along it till I passed out. Then I woke up in hospital. Some old farmer had found me, dressed my wound with an appalling mixture of leaves and flowers and wrapped a dirty bandage round me. He brought me into town. I was taken to hospital, given blood that should have gone to someone else, and I survived.'

'What about Inez?'

'I gave a statement to the police and they sent soldiers down to the old farmhouse. It was deserted. I never saw Inez again. I was found another translator and two days later I got out of bed and started work again. Babies were still being born, Jenny.'

Her head was reeling. She went over the story, tried to imagine what he must have felt. And there was one huge question still to ask. 'You thought you loved this woman, thought she loved you. How can you ever trust anyone again?'

'It can be done,' he told her. 'It's hard. But try and it can be done.'

# CHAPTER THREE

JENNY didn't see too much of Mike for the rest of the week. Sometimes it happened that way, both were busy, they just never worked together in the same place. She even wondered if he was avoiding her on purpose—not wanting to give her the chance to change her mind about the visit to Wales. But he didn't have to worry. To her slight consternation she discovered she was looking forward to the trip.

He phoned her in her room at lunchtime on Friday. 'I'm halfway through the most boring meeting I've ever been to,' he said. 'I'm a doctor, not an accountant. Just wanted to confirm details for tomorrow. Incidentally, the weather forecast seems to be good.'

'I'm looking forward to the day. Where do you want me to pick you up? And what time?'

She felt safer being brisk, efficient. He seemed to recognise this, was also efficient. 'Pick me up at my sister's place.' He gave her the address. 'And if you get there for half past eight there'll be time for a quick coffee with Sue and Sam. You're driving so I'll see to sandwiches and so on. Don't forget a warm sweater and a waterproof.'

'I have been fell-walking before,' she told him.

She replaced the receiver and smiled to herself. She was half apprehensive, half pleased. Tomorrow would be a new experience. How would she feel when the day was over? She suspected that her life might change a little.

Saturday started well, the weather was fine. It gave her an odd thrill to pull on the walking clothes that she hadn't worn for years. Today was going to be different!

She enjoyed meeting Sue and Sam again. They lived on a new estate not too far from the hospital. The garden showed signs of someone's recent care. She remembered how Sue had threatened Mike with the mowing.

Mike was packed, ready to go, but she did stop for the promised coffee. 'Don't let him go tearing ahead of you,' Sue warned. 'He's spent the past few years racing up and down mountains, he's super-fit. If you want a rest or to look at the view, you stop and enjoy yourself.'

'The slave-driver in this family is you,' Mike protested. 'The only way I could get out of more gardening is by going for a walk.'

'There's always tomorrow,' Sue promised. 'Sam! In your mouth, not on the floor.'

Jenny's breakfast times were solitary and silent. This amiable chaffing over coffee was new to her, she thought she rather liked it.

They took the fast route through the new tunnel, along the M53 and then the A55 to Wales. Mike was an easygoing passenger, relaxed about her driving and chatting happily about his life in South America. Sue enjoyed the conversation and was sorry when he

directed her off the main road and through a network
of minor roads. Here she had to concentrate on her
driving. But the scenery was something else.

Finally, after a nerve-racking drive up a steep, narrow, twisting road, he told her to stop. They parked
under trees and he led the way confidently forward.
And after ten minutes the road opened to show a long
blue lake, a circle of mountains round it.

Jenny gasped. 'This is so beautiful,' she cried.
'Why didn't I know that there was something like
this only two hours away?'

'You never know what good things you might find
till you look,' he said enigmatically. 'That's true in
life as well as in geography. Now we're going to
climb up and follow that ridge round.'

It looked high. 'We are?' Jenny asked doubtfully.

'We are. We'll take it easy, move along gently and
we'll be there before you realise it.'

It wasn't quite as easy as he'd said. She suspected
that most of the way he was holding himself back,
not moving at his normal speed. And since she was
puffing and panting, doing the very best she could,
this irritated her a little. 'I can keep up,' she said,
when she noticed him quite deliberately slowing his
pace. 'There's no need to make allowances for me.
And if you want to hare ahead, do so. I'll catch up
eventually.'

He shook his head. 'This isn't a race or a com-
petition. It's something we're doing together. Now,
just look down. See how far we've walked already.'

She did as he'd suggested and it was heartening.
The lake in the valley bottom now seemed far away,

much further than the summit ahead of them. They were getting there!

They didn't talk much on the way up. She needed all the breath that she had. But she noticed just how much he was enjoying himself, he was at home here. From time to time he would pause, stare at a distant bird or down at a plant. Then he would smile to himself. Jenny felt she was seeing a new side of the man. He was more complex than she had realised.

And finally they reached the top. The path became less steep, the wind seemed to pick up a little. And then in the distance there was another ridge, and after five minutes' easy walking they could look down into an entirely different valley. The view was magnificent!

For the moment her fatigue was forgotten. Jenny reached inside her sweater, pulled her shirt away from her warm body. This was worth the effort. And she noticed that Mike was still, as entranced as she was.

Several times as they climbed up he had taken her hand to help her over the steeper sections. Now he took her hand again, led her to the lee of a great rock. 'We can sit here and shelter a while,' he said. 'You'll find yourself getting cold quicker than you know. I think it's time for lunch.'

He spread a silver space blanket for them to sit on, then sat by her side. She rested her back against the rock, stared at the view and was entirely happy.

He poured her a mug of coffee from a metal flask, passed her a long ham roll. 'Before you ask,' he said, 'I made the lunch. I wanted the catering for this little expedition to be entirely by Donovan and company. And Sam was so fascinated by the process that I had to make him a set of sandwiches and wrap them properly in silver foil. He'll be having them about now.'

She giggled. 'You're a brilliant caterer. I'll employ you to make my lunchtime sandwiches.'

'I'd like that. What do I get as payment?'

It had been said light-heartedly but she saw something in his eyes that suggested a deeper meaning. She decided to finish their little picnic in silence. And she was hungrier than she could remember being in months.

'Why do you like it so much up here?' she asked when they had both finished.

He didn't need to think long, but pointed at the blue ridge opposite them. 'I love long views.'

'Any special reason?'

'They give me perspective. Make my troubles seem less.' He pointed to the bottom of the valley in front of them, she could just see what seemed to be two or three rows of buildings. They were of dark stone, fitted well into the landscape.

'That was an old mine, those cottages were for the mineworkers. People were born, worked and died there. Some of them didn't move very far or very often from that tiny settlement.'

She looked at him curiously. 'So what are you telling me?'

He shrugged. 'They lived happy, fulfilled lives. So should we all.'

He put his arm round her shoulders. Then he

leaned over and kissed her. At first she froze—she was shocked, she didn't know if she wanted this. But then she sighed and relaxed. 'That was nice,' she said when he stopped. Then she frowned. 'You know no one has kissed me like that in years? I'm not sure it's something I want to get used to again. In fact, I think you'd better not do it again.'

'You seemed frightened at first. Do you want to tell me, Jenny?'

She looked at him, perplexed. 'Tell you what?'

'Tell me what comes between us. The first minute I saw you, that time at the party, I was attracted to you. And we've met, and we've talked, and I think that you quite like me. But something stops you, you don't want to get involved. Could you tell me what it is?'

His voice was gentle, persuasive. She was tempted.

But then her native caution took over. 'You've only known me for a week,' she pointed out. 'Getting to know someone is supposed to be a long process.'

'Jenny, I felt I knew you the moment I saw you. And I wanted you desperately then. If you see something that you want desperately—you go for it.'

'You might. I'm not sure I want to. And how many other women have made you want them desperately? What about Inez Sanchez?' What had started as an innocent enough conversation was now drawing Jenny into places she didn't want to go. She knew her voice was shrill, showed the unease she was feeling.

After a while he said, 'I got over Inez. It took time,

but I managed. But before her there was one other woman. She had something that I always wanted, I can still feel the intensity of longing for it.'

Jenny was surprised to find that she felt disappointed. 'Tell me about her,' she said.

'Her name was Lucy Tilling. She had long blonde hair down her back. It shone, always.'

Jenny pulled at her own dark hair, aware that the pleat she had tied it into had come adrift. 'When was this?'

'About thirty years ago. She was four, I was nearly four. She was an older woman. And she had this crimson rubber ball that tinkled when it rolled and I wanted to play with it and she wouldn't let me...'

'Idiot!' she said, giggling.

'If you had a tinkly crimson rubber ball, would you let me play with it?'

He asked the question softly and she knew it was not a joke. 'I'd be afraid you'd steal it,' she said. 'Run away with it. You seem to run away with things.' She thought a minute, then said, 'Perhaps I'd say yes.'

When he kissed her this time, it was different. He wrapped his arms around her, they wriggled on the space blanket till they were lying side by side and he kissed her.

After a while Jenny opened her eyes and saw, high above her in the blue sky, a single bird flying. She felt that she was flying, too. She closed her eyes again.

She didn't know how long they lay there—minutes, hours, it didn't matter. And she didn't want to move, she was at home with his arms around her and his lips on hers. But there were things that she had to say, and suddenly they became very important.

She slid out of his grasp, sat up. 'You sit up, too,' she said. 'There are things I've got to tell you.'

'Important things? Because what we were doing was important.'

'Very important to me. Well, perhaps to you as well.'

So he sat up next to her, took her hands in his and kissed them. She remembered the first time he had done that—by her car, in the hospital car park. It had shocked her then—though she had rather liked it. And now he had done it again.

'You asked me what stopped me, why I didn't want to get involved. I suppose you guessed it was a man. A love affair.'

'Something like that,' he said cautiously.

'And you checked up on me, listened to the hospital gossip?'

He folded his arms, defensively. 'I asked Sue to find out what she could about you,' he confessed. 'I wanted things to be…right between us. I didn't want to make any awful mistakes and I didn't dare ask you. Then Sue got cross at me and said I should treat you properly.'

Jenny smiled. 'I like Sue. Anyway, I'm not going to give you the details of what happened because now they aren't important. The important thing is…what has just happened to me. Usually when I think about the past, the pain and the misery come

GILL SANDERSON                61

straight back. And I hate all men. I want nothing to
do with them, I'm not going to risk suffering more.
But now that's gone. It's as if I had been ill and I'm
cured.'

He was looking at her wide-eyed, as if he couldn't
believe what she was saying. 'And that's happened
just now?'

She shrugged. 'Perhaps it was time. But now I can
look back, I can remember that we had some good
times together and I can enjoy those memories. And
then I found out that he was two-faced, and I can
cope with that, too. He's out of my life, a memory
from the past, not a pain in the present. I can start
living again.'

She leaned towards him, took his head between
her hands and kissed him, fiercely, demandingly, on
the lips. 'You're the one who's done it, Mike, you've
been the catalyst. You've set me free.'

'If I've helped you, I want a reward.'

'Perhaps. In fact, probably. In time. But for now
that's enough emotion. I don't want to talk any more,
I just want to be.' She leaped to her feet. 'I'm so
happy I could run,' she said.

'So run. Then come back and kiss me again.'

They had to finish the walk. Mike led her along the
ridge and then they zig-zagged slowly downwards,
passing through forests of dark pine. For Jenny everything was new—the sun on the back of her neck,
the smell of resin in the forest, the splashing of the
many mountain streams. All were to be experienced

far more fully than before. And there was Mike to hold her hand.

By the time they got back to the car she was truly, happily weary. He suggested that he drive, she gladly agreed. He took her to a village pub where they had a pint of shandy each, and then he drove her back to the city. She held his hand when she could, and dozed with a smile on her lips.

He said he would drive her home and then take a taxi back to Sue's.

'No, you won't. You'll drive back to Sue's and I'm quite capable of driving the rest of the way myself. I am an independent woman, you know.'

'I do know that. How I know it. But you'll come in for tea?'

'I'll come in for a cup of tea. But Sue has enough to do coping with you and Sam. I'll not stay.'

'Things have changed between us.'

'Possibly. Well, certainly.'

'The first thing to say is that I can't see you tomorrow. I've got a family visit with Sue and Sam. It's been arranged for a while and I can't get out of it.' He sounded anxious.

'It doesn't matter. It's a good idea for me to have a bit of time to myself. I've got to get used to the new me. I want to see how I feel in the morning. There's plenty of time, Mike.'

'Not if you're feeling the way I am,' he growled, and she blushed and giggled.

They had a cup of tea at the kitchen table with Sue, and Jenny resolutely resisted her invitation to stay for the evening. 'I'm still hot, sticky and sweaty,' she said. 'If ladies can get sweaty. I need a long hot bath.'

'You had a good time, then?' Sue's voice was innocent.

'Couldn't have been better.' Jenny saw Sue glance from her to Mike, and then smile. She blushed again.

When she finally got home she decided that her flat was welcoming—but a bit shabby. Time to do some decorating. She lay in the bath, planning colour schemes, considering new furniture. She cooked herself a meal, but next morning hadn't even been able to remember what it had been. Then she went to bed and slept at once, a smile on her lips.

Next morning life was still good for her. There were two reasons—Peter had disappeared and Mike had arrived. A weight off her mind and a chance of happiness to come. What more could she want? And she knew that no longer would she have to work so hard at the hospital. Everything was planned, all the processes in place. She could afford to take things a bit easier. Live her own life. And life was good.

She was stiff after the walk. But still she decided to decorate her bedroom, it was perhaps the room that needed it most. She fetched her little ladder, dug out a scraper that she hadn't used in years and started to take off the wallpaper. While she prepared she could think of her new colour scheme. Perhaps something a bit more imaginative than the cream and beige flowers she was scraping onto the floor.

In the middle of the afternoon her phone rang. It was Mike. 'I'm taking Sam for a little walk, thought

I'd try you on my mobile. How are you? After yesterday's walk.' She could hear the uncertainty in his voice.

'I'm stiff but I'm fine. Do you know you've stopped the job, got me down from my ladder? I'm decorating.' She knew he'd respond to the cheerfulness in her tone.

'Decorating? May I see?'

'Only when it's finished. I want you to come in and see it at its best. It's my bedroom.' Then she realised what she had said. 'Don't take that too far.'

'Now, would I?' His voice lowered. 'I've missed you today, Jenny.'

'And I've missed you. But we'll meet tomorrow.'

She felt happy as she climbed back up the ladder.

On her desk next morning at work there was an envelope, with 'Jenny' written on the outside. She picked it up, there was something hard inside. Curious. She opened the envelope.

Inside was a piece of some kind of semi-precious green stone. It was carved—on one side was a smiling face, on the other a sad one. There was a leather thong attached. And it was incredibly beautiful.

She couldn't help herself, she hung it round her neck. It didn't go too well with the drab fabric of her uniform, but it was still beautiful. And then there was a knock and her door opened. It was Mike.

First he held her and kissed her. Then she opened her eyes and saw that behind him her door was still open. She pulled away frantically. 'Mike! People will see us!'

'They'll only be jealous,' he said serenely. 'And I'm doing nothing I'm ashamed of.'

'There's a time and place. Now, what's this? Did you leave it here?'

He touched the pendant around her neck, turned it so the smiling face was outwards. 'It's a present for you. For a start, the colour matches your eyes. I brought it back from a village high in Mexico, it's supposed to bring good luck.' He turned the pendant round and then back again. 'It shows that sadness can always be turned into happiness.'

She took her little mirror, looked at the reflection of the pendant. 'It's lovely,' she said.

'Will you wear it tonight? When I buy you dinner?'

She shook her head. 'I won't wear it tonight. I've got a standards co-ordinating meeting at the university. It's very important and very dreary and it'll go on for ever. What about tomorrow night?'

It was his turn to shake his head. 'I'm on call all night and John wants me to stay on or near the ward. Couple of difficult cases. In fact, I'm on call till next Friday.' He sighed. 'I never thought that my life would be messed up by timetable. True love never runs smoothly, does it? Let's just face up to it, Jenny, I'll not be really free till next weekend.'

'Then make it Saturday. I'm disappointed—but I know what doctors' work is like.' She thought a minute. 'You mentioned true love, Mike—I'm still a bit cautious. I want to take things easy at first and—'

He kissed her again. 'Find what you want and go

for it,' he said. 'And I want you so much. But I can wait—at least till next Saturday.'

They met before, of course, they worked together on the antenatal ward. It was Tuesday afternoon.

'This is Sheila,' Jenny said to Mike, pushing forward an obviously nervous girl in uniform. 'She's second year, here to gain practical experience. I wondered if we could let her perform an examination. She's watched, of course, but never actually done one.'

Mike nodded. 'Now's a good time to start,' he said. He thought for a minute. 'We've got Joan Adams, a lady who's been in labour for about four hours—we'll probably be sending her down to the delivery suite shortly. Sheila, how would you decide that your patient is about to give birth?'

Sheila thought. 'Well, there's the case history, of course. You'd know when it was likely. Then there's the waters breaking and the contractions. And then you'd perform an examination and see to what extent the uterus was dilated.'

'Good. Have you examined a dilated uterus yet?'

'Not a real one.' Sheila blushed. 'We've got this box of plastic models, all in various stages of dilatation, and we've felt all those. But I suspect they're not like the real thing.'

'Hardly at all,' Mike agreed. 'Wait here, I'll go and ask Joan if she minds you examining her.'

Every patient had to be asked if they minded being examined for training purposes. Jenny was always slightly encouraged by the fact that the great majority of people agreed. It was rare for one to refuse.

Mike came back a minute later. 'Joan says that's fine,' he said. 'This is her third child, she's quite used to maternity wards and to being examined, so she won't be nervous. So look confident, Sheila. If you look confident, you'll feel confident. Now, you're going to perform this examination, we two are just going to watch.'

Sheila gave a weak smile. 'Yes, Dr Donovan,' she said.

In fact, Sheila's bedside manner was quite good. She smiled at the patient, introduced herself and chatted for a couple of minutes. Just the procedure Jenny had said was so important. Mike observed this, nodded approvingly to Jenny. After the normal observations were taken and noted, Sheila said that she wanted to make an internal examination, arranged Joan in the proper position and snapped on the specially lubricated sterile gloves. Afterwards she frowned, but remembered in time and turned to smile at the patient. 'Thank you, Mrs Adams, all over now.' She rearranged the bedclothes.

Mike led the little group down the ward. 'A good examination, Sheila,' he said. 'You put the patient at ease and thought of her dignity—and that's important. What was the dilatation?'

Sheila bit her lip. 'Four centimetres?' she suggested.

Mike nodded. 'Not too bad. In fact, it was three centimetres. But don't worry, this is a skill that only comes with practice. But you'll get there. You'll be a good midwife, Sheila.'

Jenny could tell that Sheila was more than pleased with this praise.

And she was more than pleased with Mike. He was an excellent teacher.

It was only luck, of course, but Jenny found that the pendant Mike had given her didn't only match her eyes. It also matched the dress she had bought on impulse two weeks before. She held the pendant against the dress, and then the dress against her body. She was going to look great.

She had booked a Saturday afternoon hair appointment. Linda knew her hair and would arrange something a bit special for her. And she did. Jenny was more than happy with the result. Then she bought herself some new shoes from the arcade. As she walked away from the shoe shop she passed another small shop she'd never visited before, an obviously expensive ladies' lingerie shop.

She glanced in the window, walked on. Then she turned and looked again. No, she had quite enough underwear, no need to... She went in the shop.

It seemed she spent a fortune on not very much. But why not? She was too young to be wearing sensible underwear all the time, she was entitled to be frivolous occasionally. And she wanted to be smart right down to her skin. Down to her skin. Well, yes.

First there were things to do around the flat, she had planned quite carefully. But then it was time to change.

She took her time getting ready—had a long bath, took extra care with her make-up then slipped on her new underwear and then the dress. And, of course, the shoes, which made all the difference. Then the green pendant Mike had given her. The green of the pendant, her dress, her eyes. All went so well together.

She was a bit surprised when she looked at herself properly, there was more cleavage than she usually showed. And the scanty underwear was needed. But she knew she looked good. And because of that she felt good. She felt both exciting and excited. She sat down to wait for Mike, her heart beating faster than usual.

No male friend had been invited to her flat in the past three years. But Mike had been. She wondered what he would make of the place. It was clean, of course, but comfortable rather than smart. Still, she was changing that. She'd started on the bedroom.

When he rang her doorbell her heart beat even faster. But she remained calm, had a last check in her bedroom mirror and went to let him in. He looked so good! A lightweight fawn suit, a dark shirt. Following the fashion of the day, he wore no tie. And it gave him a slightly exotic, raffish look.

'You're dressed in green,' he said. 'I brought you this and it'll go well with green.'

He handed her a white lily, a corsage in a Cellophane box. 'Mike, it's lovely!' She reached up to kiss him—just quickly on the cheek, though. 'Come in for a minute—I'm almost ready. And you can see my flat.'

In fact, she was completely ready. But she wanted him to come into her home. It was a gesture—to herself as much as to anyone.

'I'd like to see where you live,' he said. 'There's a lot about you I want to know.'

She showed him the flat, got him to stand on the stool so he could see her view of the sea, showed him the stripped bedroom—the bed was made—and had him admire the new wallpaper she had chosen.

'I like it around here,' he said. 'In fact, I've been looking at property lists. I think I'm going to buy a flat here myself. I need somewhere with a long view—over the river or towards the Welsh hills.'

'So we'll be neighbours?'

'We'll be near each other. That'll be nice,' he said.

Then they set off. He was taking her to dinner and Jenny thought that this might be one of the most important evenings of her life.

# CHAPTER FOUR

SHE had offered to drive him again, he had refused absolutely. He would borrow Sue's car. He drove her up into the hills near Wigan, to a restaurant she had heard of but never visited. The food was superlative, but afterwards she could hardly remember a thing she had eaten. She did remember that he got her a half bottle of champagne, and had two glasses of red wine himself.

They talked, an easy, friendly conversation about families, about her work and his.

'I still want to know why you aren't married,' she said after her second glass of champagne. 'I would have thought you'd have been snapped up years ago. You've told me about Inez Sanchez and about when you were four.'

He shook his head, looked gloomy. 'My life with women hasn't always been easy,' he said. 'I've already bared my soul to you, told you the story of Lucy Tilling and the tinkling ball.'

'I appreciate your disappointment. You have had a hard time, haven't you? Tell me another story of female perversity. What dreadful woman did what dreadful thing to you?'

He thought. 'The next episode happened when I was quite mature. I wasn't a child, I was positively suave. A debonair lad about town.'

'Aged?'

'Well, thirteen. But a grown-up thirteen. And Marie Shaw was thirteen, too. We developed an understanding and she asked me if I'd like her to wear a ring. She'd already got the ring—it had come as a free gift from some girls' magazine. It was a going-steady ring, but since they weren't allowed to wear rings in school she'd have to wear it around her neck, inside her blouse, on a piece of string.'

Jenny had to giggle. 'You started your love life earlier than me.'

'I was a precocious child. Anyway, I quickly tired of Marie. Her pop groups weren't my pop groups. So I said we weren't going out together—steadily— and she wasn't to wear the ring. But she wouldn't give up. She said she would decide when things ended and I'd better watch out or she'd tell tales about what we'd done. To her mates and her mother. I pointed out that we'd done very little, she asked who would believe me. Well, I couldn't have that.'

Now Jenny had to force herself to stop laughing. 'I wonder you ever trusted a woman again. So what happened next?'

'The piece of string came undone and the ring was lost. Marie said she felt she had to tell me that, but it was a sign that our relationship was over. And a week later I saw her holding hands with a fourth-former. She'd gone up in the world.'

'Women are like that,' Jenny said.

He reached over the table, took the green pendant and dropped it inside the top of her dress. She could feel the coolness of it against her skin.

'That's my going-steady ring,' he said. 'I want you to wear it.'

She thought for a minute, then took the pendant out again. 'I'll happily wear your going-steady ring,' she said. 'But I'm proud of it, I want people to see it.'

'The dessert trolley?' a soft-footed waiter asked.

Finally the meal was finished and she said, no, she didn't want coffee. They drove home slowly, largely in happy silence, and she held his hand when it was safe. And then they were outside her flat.

She had practised this, rehearsed it even, and yet the words were still hard to speak. 'I knew you couldn't drink much because you were driving so I got something in. Would you like to come in for a drink? And I know it's silly after that wonderful meal but I got some supper, too.'

He stared straight ahead. 'I'd like that,' he said. 'But are you sure that—?'

'I'm sure,' she said quickly. 'Now, come on up before I change my mind.'

She made him take his jacket off, sat him on her couch and pulled the coffee-table towards him. 'I didn't know what to buy,' she gabbled, 'but I bought some red wine and some white wine and a bottle of whisky. Or there's coffee. And there's what they called a party platter, which needs microwaving. Just little bits of stuff. But we've just had a lovely meal and perhaps…'

Her took her hands and kissed them. He'd done that before, she wondered if it was a South American custom. 'Just sit here and relax,' he said. 'Or, better, find something to play on the machine over there, something restful. I'll open the wine and bring in a couple of glasses.'

It was good to have him take charge. 'Sinatra suit you?' she asked anxiously.

'I love Frank Sinatra. Now, don't worry. Everything will be fine.'

The DVD was already in the player, she'd been listening to it before. So she flicked the switch to turn it on. 'Come fly with me,' Frank Sinatra sang. Was that an omen?

She sat only a moment. Then she strode purposefully to the bedroom. She kicked off her shoes, slid off her tights, stepped out of her dress and hung it up. She put on her dressing-gown, long, in some silver decorated fabric. It always made her feel luxuriously comfortable. Then she lit the candles she had placed around the living room and turned off the light. Only then could she sit down and relax. What would be would be.

He came in a moment later, carrying a tray with the opened bottle of red wine and two glasses. There was rather a pleasant smell coming from the microwaved platter, and he'd brought two plates. He placed the tray on the table, sat beside her. She saw his eyes flick to her dressing-gown but he said nothing.

'I like the candles and the music,' he said. 'Makes everything restful. And this is a very nice wine.'

Restful? She didn't feel restful.

'The man in the shop recommended the wine,' she

said. 'It comes from Chile and I thought that...I didn't know if you liked...'

'I like it,' he said gently. 'I'd be happy just drinking water with you. But this is a good wine and we'll both enjoy it.'

She wasn't sure what was to come. Her heartbeat was accelerating again, she was half hopeful, half terrified. Was this a good idea, would he think she was being forward? What would he think of her? If they...well, would she disappoint him?

He seemed to guess her mood, her anxiety. He poured half a glass of wine, tasted it then offered it to her to drink. 'That is good,' he said.

She took the glass, tasted the wine. Perhaps it was good. She just didn't know.

He took the glass from her, leaned across to kiss her gently on the lips. 'There's nothing to worry about,' he said, 'no need to hurry. All good things should be enjoyed slowly. Now, we'll sit here for a while, I'll hold your hand and we can drink our wine.'

His words were calming. He leaned over again, kissed her neck. 'Just being a doctor,' he whispered. 'All I'm doing is taking your pulse. And this is a wonderful way to do it.'

'My heartbeat is fast because I'm nervous,' she confessed.

'No need to be nervous. For now we'll sit here and just be glad to be with each other.'

So they sat there together and listened to Frank Sinatra. She ate a couple of small warm somethings, though she had no idea what she was putting into her mouth. They drank and talked. He told her about medicine in Argentina, about the Amazon, about the Andes, about fighting off a condor with a six-foot wing span. And an ease crept over her.

What was to be between them was now preordained. All would be well, all would be fine. And when she knew this, she knew what she had to do. For too long she had been a victim. Now she was her own person. She would show him this.

He had taken off his jacket, thrown it over a chair. She reached over him, started to unbutton his shirt. He looked at her, said nothing. When the shirt was fully open, she slid her hand over his chest. 'Now I can feel your heart beat,' she said. 'And speaking as a nurse, I would say that yours is fast, too.'

'You've unbuttoned my shirt.' His voice was ragged, as if he wasn't sure what to say next.

'And now I'm going to take it off.' She eased the shirt upwards, slipped one sleeve from his arm and then the other. She threw the shirt on top of his jacket, and he was naked to the waist.

His body was as muscular as she had known it would be. Tentatively she leaned to touch him, sliding her hands over the powerful shoulders, the firm pectorals and the trim waist. When her fingertips grazed his nipples she heard his involuntary gasp.

'You're as sensitive there as I am,' she whispered.

'We'll have to see.' Half a threat, half a promise.

He seemed to guess what she wanted, what she needed. This was something she was doing of her own free will. It was an assertion of her right to offer herself. So as she caressed him, he remained still.

But not for long. His arm stretched around her, gathered her to him. Now his kiss was demanding, not the gentle invitation it had been before. Willingly, she opened her lips to him, lay back as he took her, his tongue seeking her sweetness. Now, for a while, he could be master. And her hands clutched his naked back.

This was so good, but she knew it was only a beginning. After a while he moved back, took her arms from around him. Then he reached for the zip of her dressing-gown, slowly drew it downwards. The hiss of the plastic zip sounded awfully loud.

He slid the gown from her, her gaze burning as he looked at her almost naked body. Then he stood, took her hands in his and lifted her to her feet. Slowly the gown fell, to become a froth of silver round her ankles.

Now it was her turn to remain still while his fingers trailed along her arms, the upper slopes of her breasts, round to her back. He must have undone it because her bra fell to the floor. She was happy to stand there, knowing the effect she was having on him. Even in the dimness of the candlelight she could see the passion in his eyes.

He threw his arms around her, kissed her again. Her breasts were crushed against him, his skin seemed to set hers on fire, she thought that never had she felt such urgency. Now the calmness, the ease they had both felt before had gone. She felt his hands on her hips, pulling at the flimsy lace there. She reached for his belt, pulled it free, so both of them could be naked. And as he clasped her to him again she felt his need for her. So good to be naked together.

He was strong. He bent, reached behind her and swept her up into his arms. Then he carried her into her bedroom.

Why had she turned down the cover, left on only the discreet bedside light?

He laid her in the bed, yet one more time looked down at her. 'Jenny,' he said, 'I want so much to…'

She guessed what he was going to say. 'It's all right, sweetheart,' she told him. 'I've taken care of things. We'll be quite safe. Now, come to bed with me.'

Perhaps it was inevitable. Earlier he had told her that they had all the time in the world, now this didn't seem to be true. His kisses had been so good but now they weren't enough. And so his lips roamed down her body, fastening on the aching tips of her breasts so that her back arched and she moaned with ecstasy.

But there still had to be more, she wanted to be his completely. Never before had she felt this need to give herself. She pulled him onto her, stared for a moment into his wide eyes and muttered, 'Now, Mike, please, I need you now.'

Then his lips were pressed to hers. And they came together as she opened herself to him, took him, received him, felt his delight and returned it.

Then it didn't take long. Her climax came as a surprise to her, she hadn't expected that so quickly. But together they reached the ultimate culmination, calling each other's name in a final statement of love.

And then lay side by side, letting the evening air cool their fevered bodies, happy just to hold hands, to be with each other.

'I don't know what to say,' he whispered to her. 'Nothing like that has ever happened to me before.'

'Nor me. I just can't find the words. So go to sleep.' She lifted one of his hands to her lips, kissed it. 'Mike, do you know how happy you've made me?'

'As happy as me,' he said.

Jenny woke first, slowly as ever. She was lying on her side, vaguely aware that things had changed in her life and that she was happy about them. It would be good to wake up today. Then she realised that there was an arm around her, holding her breast. And there was a body pressed against her back and the warmth of someone's breath on the back of her neck. She was in bed with a man. Mike.

She opened her eyes, glanced at her bedside clock. It was still early. No need to wake him, no need to get up, she could just lie here and remember the night before. And enjoy the warmth of his body next to hers.

Last night had been special. First, most importantly, it had brought her together with Mike. Second, it had reinforced her new view of herself. She was confident, assured of her femininity. She was a whole woman again.

Without thinking, she wriggled with joy. She hadn't intended to wake him but the hand on her breast tightened and he kissed the back of her neck.

'I had rather a wonderful dream,' a voice said. 'Do you want me to tell you about it?'

'If you want. I like dreams that are wonderful.' She stretched, and rolled onto her back. He leaned over her.

'Well, it involved you.'

'What was I doing? Or what were we doing?'

'I can show you if you like,' he said. 'To start with, I was kissing you.'

They were both still half-asleep, the need they had felt the night before was not so pressing. And so they had time to explore each other's bodies, to discover what gave pleasure how best they could both be happy. And then there was the inevitable crescendo, the need both to give and receive and for both another heart-pounding climax.

'Now you can kiss me one last time and then we're going to sleep again,' she said.

'If you'd like to stay in bed, I'll fetch you breakfast,' he said an hour or so later.

'Isn't that what I'm supposed to say?' Perhaps she ought to be the perfect hostess. But she was very comfortable just lying here with his arm around her.

'I'll do it. I'm a lark, not an owl. Early to bed and early up.'

'I take time to wake up.'

'You could have fooled me earlier on this morning. Ow!'

Jenny had prodded him in the waist with a hard finger. 'Earlier this morning,' she explained, 'was different.'

Then she frowned. 'I've just been thinking. What will Sue say when she finds out you didn't come home last night? And what about her car?'

'No problem. She told me I could have the car all weekend. And as to not coming home—well, I told her I might stay at the hospital.'

'And she believed you?'

'I suspect not. But we have your reputation to think of.'

She giggled. 'I'm sure it's safe in your hands.'

He leaned over in bed, kissed her on the nose. 'You've altered in the short time I've known you,' he said. 'You laugh more now.'

'It's because I'm easier with myself,' she told him. 'Because the past isn't dragging me down any more. I've lost the past, I feel free. Today is the first day of the rest of my life and I'm looking forward to it.'

For a moment he looked serious. 'Look, I know I have faults,' he said. 'I tend to rush things, when I see what I want I have to go for it straight away. It's not always a good thing. But now I want to slow down. I want to take things steadily with you, enjoy you, see where we're going. Just so long as I can be with you every spare minute you have.'

'I'll go for that, Mike. I've never felt this way before.'

'Neither have I,' he told her. 'It's so good it's frightening.'

She knew she was getting to love him, knew he loved her. But neither of them had used the actual word 'love'. It was as if they both wanted to wait, to put off making that final statement, that final commitment. The right time would come and both would know it.

And there was another feeling growing in her. She admired him. The more she saw him at work the more she saw him as a dedicated professional. He might rush things in his private life, but no one could be more careful in his professional life. And he hated to give up on anything.

The following Wednesday she invited him back to her flat for dinner. She would get back before him and cook for him. They weren't working together. She was still in the antenatal ward, he was working in SCBU—the special care baby unit.

At half past six he phoned her. His voice was flat and she frowned as she heard it. Usually he was the most cheerful of men. 'Sorry, sweetheart, I really am. But I suspect I'll have to miss dinner. I don't think I can get away from the unit.'

This wasn't too unusual. Occasionally there were emergencies and then staff just rallied round.

'If it's necessary, then it is,' she said philosophically, trying to hide her disappointment. 'What's the problem?'

'An abandoned prem baby. She was found wrapped in an old blanket in some bushes in the park. A neonate, apparently delivered there in the bushes. The police are looking for the mother, she's likely to be in a bad way. They found the placenta, there could be retained products.'

Jenny sighed. Most of her work was intensely rewarding—there was no thrill like seeing a mother

proudly accompany her new baby out of the ward—
but occasionally there were tragedies, glimpses of
lives that were ruined from the beginning.

'What's the prognosis?'

'Not good. We've done everything we can. But
she was blue when she arrived, hypothermic, in fact.
I've spent the last couple of hours working on her.
She's hypoglycaemic, low saturation, low blood sug-
ars. I've got her intubated, on a ventilator and we've
tried every combination of drugs that we can think
of. But she's regressing.'

'I'll put your dinner on standby,' Jenny said. 'Just
ring me a few minutes before you're coming. I'm
missing you, sweetheart.'

'And I'm missing you.' She could feel the depth
of feeling in his voice. 'Now, listen, and I mean this.
I want you to eat without me. No point in us both
going hungry.'

'But, Mike, I'd rather we both—'

'So would I. But, please, Jenny, have your own
meal. I'll be in touch.'

But he didn't ring her. At half past nine she did
as he had told her, ate her own meal. She didn't
enjoy it much. Then, at half past ten, she made a
decision. It took her only ten minutes to prepare a
quick cold meal. She phoned SCBU, left a message
with a nurse that Dr Donovan was not to leave the
unit. Then she drove to the hospital.

Of course, she had worked in SCBU. It was different in feel from the other wards, there were fewer
patients, less humour, less noise. At times the anxiety
in the air was almost palpable. Jenny keyed in the

code at the door, walked down the corridor, peering through the glass in the doors of the little rooms, looking at the tiniest of babies in their transparent incubators.

She found Mike in one of the rooms. He was standing at the foot of an incubator, staring sad-faced at the baby inside. Jenny tapped on the door.

He looked up, saw her and smiled. Jenny could see the joy in his eyes, he was so happy that she had come. He came to her in the corridor.

'If you can't come to me for your dinner,' she said, 'then I'll bring the dinner to you.' She offered him the bag with the three clingwrapped plates inside. 'You're working too hard, you'll be getting hungry.'

He looked from her to the bag, and then leaned forward to kiss her. 'Jenny, you're a sweetheart. My blood sugar's so low that I could... But you didn't need to bring me anything!'

'I wanted to,' she told him. 'Now, are you busy or can we go to the doctors' room so you can eat?'

He glanced back into the room. 'I guess I'm not busy,' he said.

She fetched him a mug of the coffee that was always bubbling away, and then watched with pleasure as he ate the sandwiches and salad she had made for him. He had been hungry—and when he had finished he looked decidedly better.

'Tell me about the case,' she said.

He shrugged. 'We've done everything that can be done. But it's too late. That baby's not going to make it.'

She knew that there were such cases, she had

nursed them. But his bleak words made her shiver. 'So why did you feel you had to stay? Couldn't the SHO have dealt with it?'

'I'm sure she could. But when I was in South America—when I was working in some tiny clinic miles from the nearest hospital, miles often from the next doctor—I used to get a lot of cases like this one. And they were looked after. But I tended to give them one quick examination and then…they were left to die. We didn't have many skilled staff or sometimes not many medical stores. So we had to concentrate our resources on those babies who had a fighting chance. I was directed to those. And I decided that if there was ever a case in which there was even a one in a million chance that the baby might survive and me being there could help, I'd stick around.'

'My Mike,' she said. 'Always determined to get what he wants.'

His phone rang. 'Mike Donovan here. Hi, John, yes, I suppose it is good news. What's the prognosis? Good. No, just what we expected. No, no point in her coming at all…a matter of minutes. But I'll ring back when we're certain.'

He replaced the receiver, looked at Jenny. 'They've found the mother, she was fifteen. Looks like they've got to her in time. She's going into Theatre now. She needs cleaning up but she'll survive.' He paused a moment. 'She asked after her baby. Had we found her, could she see her? I said not really.'

There was a knock on the door, a nurse looked in. 'Mike, that baby has just…'

'I'll come and look,' he said. 'I knew it would happen. And I'll switch off the ventilator.'

An hour later Jenny took Mike home. 'Sometimes you surprise me,' she told him in the car. 'All medicine is a balancing act, you've got to feel for your patients and yet distance yourself from their pain. You can't take on everybody's suffering. I thought you'd got it right—but occasionally you get very involved. Perhaps too involved.'

'It can happen,' he said. 'Like you said, medicine is a balancing act. Perhaps sometimes I do get too involved. But the other thing is worse. Not getting involved at all.'

'I think you're right.' She decided to change the subject. 'Now, you're to stay the night with me. You need to be reminded that there are good things in life.'

So he stayed. Jenny had told him that he was welcome any time but that he was still looking after Sue and Sam, and he must spend much of his time there. Of course, when Harry came back, things might be different.

And the next day was different, too. Mike had told her that Sue was coming into the hospital for her four-month antenatal check-up, and would be bringing Sam. 'Obviously I can't do it,' Mike had said, 'and, anyway, I'm doing a clinic out of the hospital.'

'I've only got paperwork then,' Jenny had told him, 'filling in five million forms and so on. So I'll go round and see her. I can play with Sam for a while.'

'They'll both like that.'

Jenny felt a bit embarrassed. She hadn't met Sue since…well, not since that first night Mike had stayed over with her. She wondered how Sue would feel about it. But she needn't have worried.

'Welcome to the family,' Sue said as they sat in Jenny's room, drinking coffee. 'I think Mike's a lucky man.'

'I think I'm a lucky woman.'

'Possibly. You know after he met you for the first time he asked me what I could find out about you?'

'Yes, he told me. I don't mind.'

'Good. Well, I'll do the same for you. What do you want to know about him?'

Jenny thought. 'There's nothing that I can't ask him,' she said after a while. 'Just one question, and that's an obvious one. I guess it's every woman's question. Why hasn't such a lovely man been snapped up before? He's told me he's had other affairs, but apart from one there was nothing too serious.'

'He had a selection of girlfriends when he was younger,' Sue said. 'But he seemed always to be the caring type. A surprising number of them stayed friendly with him after they'd split up. How he managed that, I don't know.'

'Why did he go to South America?'

'He wanted to work there, and once he makes up his mind he wants something, he goes for it. He's always been driven. Always in a hurry, always looking for something. You know that. And now he thinks he's found what he's been looking for. You.'

Jenny couldn't think of anything to say to that.

Sam had been chasing a little car round the floor. Sue picked him up and kissed him. 'One thing I will tell you about Mike,' he said. 'He'll be a wonderful father and family man. He dotes on Sam, even when Sam's being a little pig.'

'Pig! Oink oink!' Sam said cheerfully.

'What family do you have?' Sue asked.

There was silence for a moment as Jenny wondered how she should answer. Then she said, 'I have no family at all. I'm an only child. My father left my mother while I was still a baby, then my mother died of breast cancer when I was nineteen. And I've no cousins or anything like that. I've got used to being on my own.'

Sue looked appalled. 'You poor thing!' She covered Jenny's hand with her own. 'A family makes life worthwhile. Sorry! That was a terrible thing to say. Change the subject. Has he cooked for you yet?'

'No.' Then Jenny turned rather pink. 'Well, he tends to cook breakfast.'

'He can do better than that. Come to supper tomorrow night. He'll cook something Mexican. Do you like spicy food?'

'I love spicy food and I'd love to come to supper.'

'And it would be nice if you could stay the night,' Sue went on, 'then you can see what a family is really like first thing in a morning. I'm sure there'll be a bed for you somewhere. And did you know that

Sam usually goes to see his uncle first thing in the morning? While he's still in bed?'

'You're teasing me.' Jenny blushed.

'Ask him.'

When Sue and Sam were gone, Jenny set about her tedious paperwork, but there was a smile on her face. She felt happy. No, happy didn't cover everything she felt, and she'd been happy at times before. Now she felt serene. Her life had a purpose, a future. All would be well.

She had to work late to finish her paperwork and Mike came in from his clinic to look for her. She pulled him into her room, kissed him.

'That was lovely but what especially is it for?' he asked.

'For being you. And because you're going to cook for me tomorrow night at Sue's. And I'm to spend the night there if a bed can be found.'

Mike sucked in a breath. 'Well, there's my bed. But do you like kinky sex? In the morning there's likely to be three of us. You and two men.'

'Me and a man and a bit,' said Jenny. 'You can read a story to Sam and me. And what's this about a Mexican meal?'

'I shall grow a big black moustache by tomorrow night,' said Mike.

Jenny told him not to fetch her on Friday night as he had things to do. It felt a bit odd, packing a small bag with a change of clothes, something to wear at night. She wasn't going far but it felt as if she was venturing into a foreign country. She was being invited into her lover's family. That was something.

She took flowers, a bottle of the same wine she had chosen for Mike, a reading book for Sam. Sam loved books. Then she was standing outside Sue's front door and took a deep breath. Then she knocked.

Sue opened the door, smiled at her cheerfully. 'We can't go into the kitchen, the great man is busy,' she said. 'I've just got Sam off to bed so come into the living room and we'll have a glass of wine and gossip. Isn't it nice to be looked after?'

Jenny had only been in the kitchen before. As they walked down the hall Sue called, 'Jenny's here.'

'Get her a drink. Don't interfere with me in this trying time. I'm creating.'

'He gets that way sometimes,' Sue explained. 'It's the artist in him.'

Jenny loved the living room, not even the presence of Sam's toys in a large basket could detract from its elegance. Sue poured her a drink, pointed to a rug on the wall. 'Mike sent us that from Yucatan. Isn't it glorious?'

It was indeed. It glowed, throbbed with colour, seemed to light up the whole room. 'Gorgeous,' said Jenny.

'*Señora* and *Señorita*! Soon I shall be a-doing the Mexican meal for the most beautiful ladeez. Please to sit at table.'

Jenny turned, her mouth open in shock. And then she giggled. Mike was dressed in black trousers and a white shirt. There was a vast straw sombrero at a rakish angle on his head, a red serape across his shoulder. And worst—or best—of all, he was wearing an apparent black Zapata moustache.

'So that's what you wanted my eye make-up for,' Sue said severely. 'Mike, you'll put us off our dinner.'

'Just trying to inject a bit of ethnic local colour,' Mike said dolefully. 'Jenny, have you noticed that only men are true romantics?'

'I'm a midwife,' Jenny said. 'I've seen where true romance gets women.'

It was a wonderful meal. Spicy but not too hot. They had a variety of first courses—a shrimp ceviche, a green salad and a lettuce and grapefruit salad. There were ingredients that Jenny recognised, but the sauces and the spices were different.

Then they had the threatened chicken in chocolate—and to Jenny's amazement it was good. And the bean and vegetable accompaniment was equally tasty. To finish there was mango and tequila ice cream with banana bread.

'That was so good,' Jenny gasped when she had finally finished. 'Does everyone in South America eat like that?'

'Not all the time. But they pride themselves on making the most of local ingredients. What's called Mexican cooking in this country is often a poor imitation of the real thing.'

Jenny was not surprised that he was a good cook. She had seen the care he had taken of patients, she'd guessed he might be the same about other things.

It was a relaxed, enjoyable evening, Jenny felt that she was part of a family. There was a minor argument at the end of it as everyone felt they had to wash up. They compromised, all three did it together. And shortly afterwards they went to bed.

Jenny slept with Mike. She had wondered how she would feel in another woman's house, another woman's bathroom. But she felt fine. She liked being part of a family. It made her feel loved and wanted— and belonging.

# CHAPTER FIVE

NEXT morning Jenny's idyllic life was blasted. Later, much later, she could look back on that black day and wonder that such a little mistake could alter two lives so much.

It was a fine morning, Mike suggested that they take Sam for a walk in the park and give Sue a chance to catch up on housework. Jenny thought that a bit unfair—but Sue leapt at the idea.

So Jenny, Mike and Sam walked down the road, turned to where the park stretched in front of them. Sam, for once not slippery, walked between them, each of them holding one of his hands. He loved being swung, shouted with delight. With a catch in her throat Jenny wondered if, in not too many years, she and Mike might be swinging their own child between them. It was a thought that both frightened and fascinated her.

The shoelace of one of her sensible shoes came undone. She stopped to tie it and as she pulled, the lace broke. 'You tie a knot in it,' Mike said. 'Sam and I will go across the road and buy the usual weekend ice cream. What flavour would you like?'

Jenny settled for a simple vanilla. Then she sat on a bench to fasten her lace.

She saw it all happening. Mike and Sam were at the ice-cream van, Mike feeling in his pocket for money. Just for a second he let go of Sam's hand. Sam turned, saw her on the bench, shouted, 'Auntie Jenny.' Then he ran to her. Straight across the road.

For Jenny, life suddenly seemed to be in slow motion. She saw Mike turn, see what was happening, saw the horror on his face as he realised it was too late to do anything. She saw a car coming towards Sam, even saw the panic on the old lady driver's face. She couldn't stop or swerve. She saw Sam realise that he had done something very wrong—and slip. The car would hit him.

At school Jenny had been a sprinter. She had been quite good, but had given it all up when she'd started nurse training. Now sheer terror made the adrenalin surge through her system and half-forgotten abilities came back.

She ran towards Sam. Quick, short, initial steps, arms thrust high in the air to pull her forward. Body inclined, almost parallel to the ground, to get all the drive from the thighs. Forget the car bearing down on her. She had to get to Sam.

She reached down, grabbed Sam's tiny body, threw it forward. Vaguely she heard the screech of brakes, but she knew it would be too late. Then there was a bang, a crunch as something hit her legs. No time for pain. Just instant blackness.

Something was wrong, very, very wrong. Something broken? She wasn't sure where she was or what was happening, but something was very, very wrong. She didn't want to open her eyes, but perhaps she ought to. And why was she lying down and what was that

noise—someone calling her name? Then she came
back to full consciousness and wished she hadn't.

She was lying on her back, the ground was hard.
Her head hurt, it hurt a lot. So did her arm. And her
back and her legs were…funny.

'Jenny, Jenny, can you hear me?' A voice, hoarse
with anxiety. Mike's voice. She remembered him.
She opened her eyes to see him looking down at her
with an expression of such desperation that she had
to feel sorry for him. And there were other faces
looking down, sympathetic, curious faces.

Then she remembered. It took a while before she
could make her mouth work. 'Sam? How's Sam?'
she managed to croak.

'He's fine. There's a lady here holding him and
she won't let go. Jenny, are you OK?' She could tell
he knew it was a foolish question but he'd had to
ask it.

'I have felt better,' she said.

It had always been easy to read his face—he
couldn't keep his emotions from showing. And now
she could see two sides of his character warring. He
was the desperate lover, the man she loved. There
was the gleam of tears in his eyes. And he was a
doctor and she, for the moment, was his patient. And
the doctor had to win.

She saw the effort of will he made to hold back
his emotions, to let his professional skills take over.
She was a patient, he was a doctor.

'Don't try to move anything, just lie there. We've
sent for an ambulance. It'll be here very soon and
you'll be all right.'

She could feel a trickle of warmth and damp on the side of her head, obviously it was bleeding. Someone offered him a handful of tissues, he pressed them to the side of her head. Then she saw him peering into her eyes. She knew what he was doing, looking for different-sized pupils to see if she was concussed. She didn't feel concussed. Not that she knew what being concussed felt like.

He turned away from her and she heard him say to someone, 'Get more of those tissues and hold them against that bleeding on the leg. Hold, don't press.'

Perhaps the person did as he was told. But Jenny couldn't feel anything.

He turned back to her. 'You've cut your head, but where else hurts, Jenny?'

She had to think about that. 'My head hurts most. And my arm. And my legs feel…funny.'

'Don't try to move! Don't move your head, any part of you.'

But, without thinking, she tried to turn to look at him—and shrieked with the pain.

'Jenny! Keep still! Now, where was the pain?'

'My arm hurts so much!'

She felt his fingers slide along her arm and then, very gently, lift it so it rested across her chest. It still hurt but the pain was bearable. 'It should be easier there,' he said. 'Now, keep still.'

He felt the side of her neck, gently probing the top of her spine. Then he touched the side of her head—that hurt, too. But she heard his grunt of satisfaction. 'I doubt your skull is fractured,' he said. 'But keep your head still till we can get a cervical collar on you.'

Sometimes she just wanted to shut her eyes. Other times she opened them and stared at him. There was still that conflict of feelings on his face. He had to be the dispassionate doctor, doing what was best for an injured person. But he was also a lover, trying to grapple with the shock, the horror, the anxiety of seeing his loved one so suddenly thrown into danger.

She was fully conscious now, feeling the full pain of her injuries. And now there was something so bad that she didn't want to mention it. Perhaps if she kept silent it would go away. But she had to tell Mike. He was a doctor.

'Mike! What's wrong with my legs?'

'I'm not sure,' Mike said. 'You might have… might have injured your spine.' She knew what that could mean. She couldn't help it. She jerked and her arm slid down her chest. Then there was pain such as she had never experienced before. Jenny fainted.

There were voices, official sounding, voices that seemed to carry authority. 'Please, stand back, everyone. We need to get the ambulance closer.'

Mike looked up. There were two policemen—no, a policeman and a policewoman. And behind them the white of an ambulance with the two green-coated paramedics climbing out. He hadn't even heard the siren.

It was one of the hardest things he had ever done, but he stood back. He might be a doctor but these

men were paramedics, trained specifically to deal
with this kind of incident. One of them knelt by
Jenny, the other looked at him neutrally. 'What can
you tell us, sir?'

What did they really need to know? Mike forced
himself to concentrate. What would he want to know
if she had just come into A and E? 'The lady is aged
thirty-two, in good health. No allergies. This morning
she had a light breakfast. Her breathing appears to
be patent, she doesn't appear to be concussed, she
was speaking clearly a moment ago. I saw…' Mike
swallowed. For a moment the words just wouldn't
come. But they had to! 'I saw the accident. She was
struck by a car at hip level and thrown several feet.
She struck her head as she fell, the impact was not
too great. There's a fractured arm…and…no feeling
in her legs.'

He saw the paramedic's raised eyebrows and said,
'I'm a doctor.'

'Then you'll know what we have to do, Doctor.
Do you know the lady?'

'Yes,' said Mike. 'I'll come in the ambulance with
her.'

He stood back and watched carefully. Sterile
dressings were applied to Jenny's head. A cervical
collar was put on—always a good precaution. Then,
with infinite care, she was lifted and placed onto a
long spinal board. Her entire body was immobilised,
the fractured arm strapped to her chest.

Jenny moaned as they lifted her and her pain-filled
eyes flicked open. 'You'll be all right in a moment,

love,' one of the paramedics soothed. 'We've got gas and air in the ambulance, that'll take away the pain.'

'I want Mike.'

'The doctor? He'll come with us.'

'Were you with the young lady, sir? We'd like to take a statement from you when it's convenient.'

It was the policewoman. Mike realised that there were other things he had to see to. All he'd thought about so far had been Jenny. 'I saw everything,' he said. 'I'll give a statement later.' And being a fair and honest man, he had to add, 'It wasn't the car driver's fault. There's a little boy—Sam there. I brought him out and—'

'We'll take him home,' the policewoman said. 'And you'll wait for us at the hospital?'

'I'll be there,' said Mike.

It didn't seem right to go into her own hospital. But it was the nearest and it had an excellent A and E department—in fact, Sue worked there. Not today, though.

The ambulance crew had radioed ahead, and she was met by a medical team, crashed straight through for immediate attention in the resus room. Mike remained by her side as long as he could—eventually he was told that he was to leave the room while they conducted the preliminary examination.

They put in an IV line as she'd lost some blood. There was the danger of internal bleeding from her fractured arm.

Mike was with her when the portable X-ray machine was brought through. The technician seemed to be taking far more pictures than was necessary. 'They want to check everything,' Mike told her. 'Just to make sure.'

She was in no great pain, she had been given morphine. She drifted in and out of consciousness, not really bothered about what was happening to her. Always, she was aware that Mike was with her. And that meant that everything would be all right.

'They've got you stabilised,' Mike said, in one of her periods of consciousness. 'For the moment you've just got to rest. But soon Mr Spenser is going to look at you. He'll put things right.'

'I want you with me,' said Jenny.

Everyone knew that Mr Spenser was an important man. Even Jenny, in her vague state, knew that he was very important. He was very tall, had a thin face and half-moon glasses. He was wearing a brilliant white shirt, a tightly knotted tie. Jenny had seen him, never spoken to him. He was one of the ablest neurosurgeons in the country. What no one had told her was that he was also a very kind man.

He bent over her later that day and said, 'I know you're one of our own, Jenny. You're a tutor and a midwife. I've heard of you. I'm going to see to you personally, see that you get the best we can offer.'

And she had burst into tears. Kindness was hard to take and she was terrified.

He patted her on the shoulder and said, 'We're arranging for you to be admitted onto one of my wards. First, I'm going to give you an injection of methylprednisone. There's a lot on inflammation round your sacral vertebrae and I want to get it down.

We have your X-rays, CT and MRI scans and in a few minutes we'll be off to the theatre to see if we can stick you together again. And when we've had a good look we'll know better what we have to deal with. Happy with that?'

'Whatever you say, Mr Spenser. My legs are paralysed. How badly damaged is the spinal cord? Is it severed?'

It was a question she knew he hadn't wanted. But he gave her an honest answer. 'No, it isn't severed. There should be some possibility of movement—eventually. You're a young, healthy woman, and with care and luck we should be able to fit you together again. In a year or so, if all goes well, this all could be just an unhappy memory.'

'A year or so. And that's if things go well. Could they…could they go badly?'

'Nothing is certain in medicine, Jenny.'

'And you'll tell me honestly what you find?'

His eyes were full of pain. 'In these cases I'm always honest, Jenny, otherwise the torment is worse. Now, I understand you've been prepped. I'll see you in Theatre.' He left her little side room and she turned to Mike.

All this time she had been aware of Mike in the background. He knew better than to interfere, to ask questions. But he was there, and she was glad. Whenever there was a pause in the attention she was getting he came to her side and held her hand. He brushed aside her hair, kissed her forehead.

'This is worse for you than it is for me,' she had whispered.

'Hush, sweetheart. Just remember...I'm here for you.'

This was a new Mike. So far in every situation they had met together he had been competent, in charge, knowing what to do for the best. Now this wasn't the case. Decisions were out of his hands, he could only watch and hope. And he was terrified by that.

Jenny loved him more for it. He was human after all.

It was evening, she'd been sedated and was drifting in and out of sleep. 'What happened to Sam?' she asked drowsily.

'He's fine. A nice policewoman took him home. Sue has been phoning me and leaving messages every half-hour, she's distraught about you.'

'I'm going to be fine. Don't worry about me. Tell her not to worry.'

But she could see his face and knew that wasn't possible. He would worry and so would Sue.

A nurse came in, smiled at them both. 'The anaesthetist will be here in a minute,' she said. 'But first there are some consent forms to sign for the operation, and I've got to explain them to you.'

'I'm a nurse and a midwife here. I know what the forms mean. I've given them out myself. Just let me sign them.'

The nurse sighed. 'It's protocol. You don't have to listen, but I've got to explain.'

She turned to Mike, said with a kind smile, 'I know you're a doctor here but you're involved with the patient. It might be a good idea if you waited somewhere else until Mr Spenser's finished. You'll do no good to her or yourself just hanging round until then.' She paused a minute and then said, 'You know, in situations like this, often the best thing to do is work. If you can.'

Mike hesitated, then nodded. 'All right. If I leave you my bleeper number will you call me the minute she comes out of Theatre?'

'I'll do that. Now, off you go! You're interfering with patient care.'

Mike came over, kissed Jenny's forehead. On her bruised cheek she felt the drop of a tear. Then he was gone. She heard him exchange a couple of words with someone just outside. A woman walked in wearing scrubs. 'Hi, I'm Tina Land, your anaesthetist. A couple of words before we start…'

In a hospital, word got around fast. Mike walked over to the obs and gynae wards—and the minute he entered there was a barrage of anxious enquiries. Doctors, nurses, students, midwives, technicians—all wanted to know how Jenny was. Mike hadn't quite realised just how popular she was. And that only made him feel worse.

He went to the doctors' room, looked for the senior registrar who was on duty. It was Ellie Crane. She was in the antenatal ward, checking an unexplained rise in a mother-to-be's temperature. Mike waited till she had finished, answered all her questions about Jenny and then said, 'I'm waiting till Jenny comes out of surgery. Can you find me some work till then? I need to be occupied.'

Ellie studied him for a moment and asked bluntly, 'Are you up to it? We don't want mistakes made.'

'I'm up to it. I just want something simple—like an SHO's job. How about the one on the delivery suite?'

'Fine. Go and tell him you'll do his job for a while. He can study, he needs to. But he stays in the building so he can take over when you leave.'

'Thanks, Ellie.'

There were three women in advanced labour when he arrived at the delivery suite. For the next three hours he did the simple but important tasks that the junior doctors handled. There were the observations, the help when requested by the midwives, the notes to write up and the mums to smile at. Usually these days he was only called to the delivery suite when there was an emergency. But he found the work that he was doing, coping with simple, straightforward births, was satisfying. It even took his mind off Jenny. A bit.

After some time he was bleeped. Jenny had come out of Theatre.

Mike briefed the SHO. Then officially he handed his work over and went back to the neurological theatre.

Mr Spenser was sitting in his scrubs. He was drinking a cup of coffee and looked tired. 'You're not officially related to Miss Carson,' he told Mike, 'and to be perfectly proper, I shouldn't talk to you until I've spoken to her. But I will. Did you see the X-rays, the CT and the MRI scans?'

'I saw them. The sacral vertebrae were in a mess.'

Mr Spenser nodded. 'It was bad when we got inside. But the spinal cord isn't completely severed. We've done what we can, cleaned up the bone chips and seen to the inflammation. What I'm going to have to tell her is that…well, there's still hope. She'll be in a wheelchair for quite some time. We didn't try to see to her arm—that can wait a few days.'

'What's the worst possible prognosis?' Mike asked.

'Convalescence could take an awful long time. As I said, a long period in a wheelchair. And if things don't work the way we want them to…perhaps she'll never walk again.'

'You're not going to tell her that tomorrow!'

'No,' Mr Spenser said. 'That possibility is a bit of news that can wait. Now, do you want to see her?'

Of course, he had seen people coming out of surgery before, knew that the drawn white face was just the result of anaesthesia. But she didn't look like the Jenny he knew so well.

'She won't come really round now till morning,' the nurse there said. 'She may not even know you. Why not go home and get some rest? You look terrible yourself. You need to be strong for her tomorrow.'

So he kissed her white cheek and decided that was the best thing to do.

Mike stood outside the hospital and stared at the dark sky. It was late. He didn't know what to do. For the past twelve hours he had thought solely of Jenny, had spent most of his time no more than a few feet from her. Now she was completely out of his care.

This morning now seemed so far away. He had walked out with Sam and Jenny, the weekend had stretched in front of them, a time of happiness. They had been planning a trip to Wales, this time taking Sue and Sam on a picnic. How things had changed.

Where to go, what to do now? He may as well go home. There were always taxis outside the hospital.

He didn't feel any better when he walked into the house. There was his sister sitting in the kitchen, clutching a sleeping Sam. Her cheeks were tear-streaked.

'How is she? I've just phoned the hospital again. They say she's had an operation, is in no danger and she'll have a treatment assessment tomorrow.'

'That's about right. They'll tell you nothing because there's nothing to tell.'

'Right. How long since you had anything to eat?'

He stared at his sister as if he didn't understand the question. Then he thought about it—nothing since breakfast. 'I'm just not hungry,' he said.

'You're going to eat anyway. You need to. If you want, you can take Sam to bed. He got up and I just wanted to hold him, couldn't bear to take him back. But I'm better now.'

'Is Sam OK?'

Sue gave him a wan smile. 'He's fine. He enjoyed his trip in the police car with the policewoman. She was good, by the way. Very reassuring.'

So Mike took his nephew in his arms and carried him up to bed. As he laid the little body in his bed,

Sam stirred a little, but he didn't wake. Mike looked down and relived the horror of the moment when he'd realised that Sam was out of reach, that the car was going to hit him and there was nothing whatsoever that he could do. Then he went down to the kitchen.

He tried to talk but Sue told him to keep quiet, to eat first. She had cooked him a lasagne. So he did as he was told and found that he was ravenous. Sue sat at the kitchen table, looking at him.

When he had finished she fetched the brandy bottle and a glass, poured him a large drink. He sipped the fiery liquid. He didn't exactly feel better but the numbness and the feeling of inadequacy left him. Now he could cope.

'Right,' Sue said. 'I want you to tell me what happened. I've had a cautious version from the policewoman and a semi-coherent one from you over the phone. Now, you tell me properly.'

So he told her. And finished by saying that if he had held on to Sam, everything would have been all right.

Sue shook her head. 'No. He's Slippery Sam. It could have happened to anyone. Keep that in mind.'

She poured herself a glass of brandy and gave him a refill. 'After this we both go to bed,' she said.

He had a shower, went to his bedroom. Under the pillow on one side was Jenny's nightdress, she had spent last night with him. He took the nightdress, buried his head in it. It smelt of her, of the warmth of her body. He climbed into bed, still clutching the scrap of white silk.

He could have taken a sleeping pill, he had some locked up in his doctor's case. But he didn't. He knew he had to subdue his whirling thoughts himself, not with chemical assistance.

Had it been his fault? Was there any point in thinking about fault? Whatever, Jenny was in hospital. He kept on telling himself that it was foolish to anticipate what might not be, to suffer unnecessarily. But he was a doctor—he knew. He had seen the X-rays, the scans. She might be paralysed for life. No, he mustn't dwell on that. He must wait and see.

Then he thought of the woman who loved dancing, who loved walking. Again he made himself think of something else. Hope for the best.

He remembered the first time he had seen her, remembered the stolen kiss. He remembered their meetings since, wondered at how rapidly they had come to know each other.

Not just to know each other! To love each other! He had been foolish in saying they would take time to get to know each other. He had been content to live in the present, not realising that the future could never be foretold. He should have told her he loved her. He wanted to spend the rest of his life with her.

He thought that she loved him. Well, that was more than a start. Now he could go to sleep.

Mike was there when she woke next morning. Jenny saw him sitting by her bed, looking down at her.

It was hard, waking up. First there was the vague feeling that something was not quite right. Then there was the pain. She felt battered. Then there was the memory of yesterday, the sickening realisation that she was...well, she was in hospital. She couldn't help it, she moaned. And then he was taking her hand, raising it to his lips to kiss.

'It's all right, sweetheart. Everything will be all right. Just lie there, don't try to move. I'm with you.'

Then she didn't need to talk. She lay there perfectly still, her hand in his. Mostly she kept her eyes shut, but when she opened them there he was, still looking down at her. She took strength from his very presence.

There seemed to be more confidence in his smile, he was not the horrified man she had seen yesterday. And this, too, gave her strength. If Mike was there, things couldn't be too bad.

A little later a nurse came in, said that in five minutes she was going to turn Mike out while she helped Jenny wash.

'You've got a job to go to,' Jenny told him. 'You'll be needed on the wards.'

'They know I'm likely to be late. John Bennet told me to take as much time off as I needed. He'll be in to see you later. And there's been all sorts of messages from the rest of the staff. You're popular. Everyone wants to come and visit.'

Jenny thought for a moment. 'Pass me that mirror from over there,' she said.

'What do you want a mirror for? You're fine and—'

'The mirror, Mike!'

So he passed it to her. She was a nurse, she knew what to expect. And her face felt bruised. But even so she winced as she saw the extent of the swelling on her face, the dressing on her head where the hair had been cut away. 'I don't want to see anyone,' she said. 'That is, I don't want anyone to see me.' She added, 'Apart from you and one or two others.'

'Fair enough. As I said, John Bennet said I could take as much time off—'

'I'm seeing Mr Spenser some time this morning. I can't think until then. I'll feel better if I know that you're working, I don't want you just hanging around. It'll upset me and it'll upset you.'

'But, sweetheart, I—'

'Off you go, Mike, the nurse is coming in to wash me now. You know you'll be told as soon as there's any news.' She smiled. 'I've got a confession to make. On the consent form they got me to fill in, I put you down as my next of kin. Hope you don't mind.'

'Consent form? I'm…I'm glad you did that.' Then the nurse came back in, and he was gone.

But he was back when Mr Spenser came round to see Jenny. The nurse bleeped him, he had asked her to. He waited outside while Mr Spenser made his examination and then came in to hear what the man had to say.

The neurologist said he was reasonably happy with the result of the previous day's operation, but Jenny must realise that she had been very badly injured, the result was still uncertain. Time would tell. The arm he would see to in a few days' time. Jenny must try not to worry and he'd be in to see her tomorrow.

Now he was going to prescribe analgesics. He wanted her to sleep.

Then he left.

Mike came over to hold her hand and kiss her cheek.

'I'm a nurse,' she said, 'I understand doctor-speak. Mr Spenser suspects that this operation won't be a success, doesn't he? I'm going to be paralysed?'

There was nothing Mike could say and she was sorry she had caused him to worry again. 'Now,' she said, 'I think I know what you've been through in the past couple of days so I'm giving you an order. I've been prescribed a tranquilliser. I don't want to see you till tomorrow. I'm going to sleep all day.'

'But I want to be here with you, for you!'

'You can't help me sleep. If anything, you'll make it harder. Mike, come and kiss me and then off you go.'

'But, Jenny, I—'

'I mean it! Look, I'm the ill one here, I'm the one who gets what she wants. So go!'

'I'll leave the nurse my number,' he said as he left, 'if you want me—any time of night or day.' But she didn't phone.

Mike was there again when Jenny woke the next day, but was soon hustled out again by the nurses. They had things to do with Jenny, but suggested he come back at midmorning after the consultant's round and spend a little time with her. Jenny felt surprisingly calm. Perhaps it was the effect of the pills she was taking. Certainly the pain had been reduced to a vague discomfort. But whatever it was, she knew that her mind was clear.

He kissed her, as he always did, gently, so as not to hurt her face. Then he sat by her bed, took her hand.

'There are things that I've got to say to you,' she said, 'things to sort out now. First of all, we face up to the situation. My legs are paralysed. In a few weeks we'll know if they're ever going to mend properly. If they don't then I spend the rest of my life in a wheelchair. Correct?'

He wasn't expecting this brutal summing-up, winced as he heard it. But he realised that this was the way she had to tackle things. 'Correct,' he said. 'But, Jenny, I—'

She had to make it clear what she wanted. 'We're dealing with facts now, not emotions,' she said. 'And we start with how you're feeling.'

'Me! You're the one who's been hurt.'

'Quite so. And I don't want you suffering for me. I can suffer on my own. The last thing I need from you is a long face. What I need is big smiles and confidence. Now, let's get something out of the way and then we can get on with life. Do you feel guilty at letting Sam go and then me getting hurt saving him?'

'Of course I do! I've been over that moment a thousand times and each time I feel sick at what I did. I knew what Sam was like, I knew there was a road behind us, I knew—'

'Mike! This is doing no good! It wasn't your fault, and I should know. Now, say to yourself that it wasn't your fault. If it's necessary, say it a hundred times. But say it until you believe it. Because you're no use to me if you're crippled with guilt.'

He stared at her in silence, and for a moment she wondered if she had gone too far. Then his white face broke into a reluctant smile. 'Jenny,' he said, 'you're a woman in a million.'

'Probably,' she agreed. 'Most women are. Now, say it. Say it out loud and believe it. "It wasn't my fault."'

'It wasn't my fault,' he said.

'Good. That's settled and you should feel better. Now, come here and hug me.'

That afternoon she had several visitors, not only other members of staff but also the students she was teaching. Eventually the ward sister said she was going to ration the visitors. 'You're tiring my patient! Work out some kind of rota among yourselves. Or if you want, I'll find you some work to do on the ward.'

Sue came in the evening, Mike stayed at home to babysit Sam. Sue bent to kiss her and said, 'I'm not going to get emotional.' Then she laid her head on the bed and wept. 'I'm so sorry this happened,' she sobbed.

Jenny reached down and stroked her back. 'It's not that bad,' she said. 'I've got a fighting chance.'

'Mike told me all about it. I know that accidents happen. But one thing I'll never forget. But for you, Sam would be dead. Jenny, I'll never forget that.'

Jenny felt rather embarrassed. 'It wasn't really a decision on my part,' she said. 'I just did it. And I'm glad I did. Now, would you like a chocolate? I've been collecting all sorts of presents.'

When the day ended she felt exhausted. And when her light was put out and she was alone, she wept silently into her pillow. But she had to remain strong, she knew it was the only way she could cope. And there was Mike. The thought of him made her smile through her tears.

A week passed. She had an operation on her arm, a plate and screws fitted. It would be wrong to say that she got used to not being able to move her legs— but she learned to cope with it. Mike came to see her three or four times a day, kept up his promise to remain cheerful. And there were always other visitors—she hadn't realised just how many friends she had. Mr Spenser came to chat and check on her. And Jenny managed to keep her fear hidden from everyone.

Sue was a regular visitor and at the end of the week she said, 'I hear that they're talking about discharging you. Mike says that you live in a top-floor flat and that there's no lift. So that decides it, there's to be no argument. You're moving in with us. I'm a nurse, Mike's a doctor, we can cope easily. You're to come as soon as they let you out.'

Jenny smiled. 'I'd like that,' she said. 'It's a long time since I've been part of a family.'

A week later the occupational therapist came to teach Jenny how to deal with her life. 'This is not a disability, it is a condition,' Alice, the therapist, said.

'And I'm going to show you how to deal with your condition.'

The first lesson was showing Jenny how to wriggle out of bed and into a chair. It was surprising how weak she had become after her stay in bed. Of course, she knew about this—she had even lectured about it. But to experience it was something different.

Then she discovered what she could do—and not do—in a wheelchair. Most people, of course, had two arms to manage with. She had only one. Her first trip down the ward was a voyage of discovery. 'I'm going to spend the rest of my life going in circles,' she said.

Mike was behind her. 'While you're on a flat and polished floor like this,' he said, 'you can push yourself. I'm going to stroll along with my hands in my pockets. Outside and up hills, I don't mind lending a hand.'

Then there was her first solo visit to the specially constructed bathroom on the ward. It felt so good to be able to wash herself—and how she wished she could get in the shower.

For an awful lot of this time Mike was with her. She had made him promise that in no way would he neglect his patients—and she didn't think that he did. But he found occasion to visit her many times a day.

When she got a little stronger she knew there was something that she had to say to him. For a while their relationship had to alter slightly. Being in a wheelchair, having an uncertain future, made things different. And if he didn't realise that, she would have to make him.

'Listen, sweetheart,' she said to him, 'we were going places before this thing happened to me. I suspect you were making plans and I've a good idea what they were. But we had an agreement. It was your idea. We were going to take things easy for a while. Get to know each other, enjoy just being together. Well, that's the way I want things to continue.'

'But things aren't the same! They've changed and I want to—'

'Poor Mike! The man who has to do everything in a rush! I'll teach you how to wait, young man.'

'I don't want to wait,' he growled. 'I want to see you just a bit better than you are and then I—'

'Mike! No more talk of the future until I'm out of this wheelchair! And if I'm different…that is, if I—'

'It'll make no difference whatsoever to my feelings for you.'

'It might make a difference to my feelings for me! So promise! We take things easy, OK? I want no heavy emotional scenes, no mad promises about what you'll do for me. Even if they are true. Mike, I mean this! Don't make me argue with you now! I just need a period of calm.'

She knew he could tell that she was determined. And so, with bad grace, he said, 'Well just for now, then.' And she had to be content with that.

And finally she was discharged. Alice had been around to Sue's house to recommend what changes might be needed and the district nurse would come at regular intervals.

Mike had wheeled her out into the grounds several times already, but it gave her an extra thrill to be taken outside and know that she was leaving. She had worked in hospitals for years now, but for the first time she thought she fully understood how patients felt when they said that they were bored with their stay.

She blinked as he wheeled her outside. 'My new car,' Mike said. It was a people carrier.

'I thought you said you were going to get a little runabout,' she said. 'Just big enough for four.'

'Changed my mind.' He pushed her to the passenger side and opened a large sliding door. 'Now, see if you can climb out of the wheelchair and into the car.'

It was a bit of a struggle, but she could. And it was far easier than she had expected. Mike beamed at her. 'There's a lot of room in the back for your wheelchair,' he said. 'No need to collapse it or anything.'

'Mike! Did you buy this monster just to suit me?'

'I've always wanted a really big car,' he said. 'And I've always wanted a red car. So now I've got both in one.'

'Seems like a bargain,' she muttered.

It was good to get to Sue's house. Mike had arranged for a wooden ramp to be placed down the front steps and for a similar ramp from the living room through the French windows into the garden so she could get out on her own.

The ground floor had been rearranged. Jenny could wheel herself into the bathroom. A small room had been converted into a bedroom and a wardrobe and a chest of drawers put in. Jenny looked at the single bed and whispered to Mike, 'I don't think much of that. Only big enough for one.' Mike looked suitably disconcerted.

Jenny had written out a list for Mike and he had taken Sue round to her flat and fetched the clothes, books and papers that she needed. They were neatly set out in her new bedroom.

Jenny saw the thought and care that had been taken for her and bit her lip. She wasn't going to cry. But people were good to her.

Then Sue came in, having fetched Sam from the childminder's. Sam was fascinated by the wheelchair so Jenny sat him on her lap and took him for a ride. Then she climbed out of the chair, sat on the couch and let Sam have a ride on his own.

''S lovely,' he shouted. 'Mummy, can I have one of my own?'

Sue had to turn away to hide her tears.

But it was going to work. Jenny knew she would settle in. When she said that she was going to bed that night, Sue offered to come in and help her. 'No need, thanks. I've practised, I can manage. I'm independent.'

Mike tapped on her door later. He came in and hugged her, gave her a gentle goodnight kiss.

And that set a pattern.

# CHAPTER SIX

ON THE ward Jenny had been given sleeping pills to enable her to sleep. Now she had to manage without. And she knew it was a good idea, she didn't want to become addicted to them. She hardly slept at all and when she did sleep she was tormented by memories of the last few microseconds before the accident. She thought she could see the bonnet of the car bearing down on her, feel that first crunch, hear the sound of bones snapping. Then she woke, moaning to herself, her body covered in sweat.

Mike came in early next morning, brought her a small glass of orange juice. He frowned down at her, put his hand on her forehead.

'How did you sleep? Was the bed comfortable?'

She was too tired to try to lie to him. 'The bed is fine. But I just…I kept on remembering the accident and then I was afraid again.'

'Jenny, you've had a very serious accident. Your mind took a beating as well as your body, you're suffering from post-traumatic stress. It will pass but perhaps you should speak to Mr Spenser about it.'

'Perhaps you're right, we'll see.'

Sometimes she had visions, nightmares in the day while she was awake. She thought of herself, her friends being involved in the worst of accidents. And tears would come to her eyes, her body would shiver and she just knew that the worst things in the world were going to happen. They never did. But she knew they would.

One afternoon she was sitting in the sitting room in her wheelchair, trying to read. She was keeping a vague eye on Sam. Sue was in the kitchen. And suddenly there was a vision of what might have happened if she hadn't got to Sam in time. She saw the little body rocking into the air, the small bones shattering, the blood pouring.

'Sam, Sam, come here,' she moaned.

Obediently, he came. She pulled him onto her lap, wrapped her arms around him and tried to take strength from the fact that he was alive. And that was how Sue found them five minutes later.

'Sam! Jenny, is he all right?'

Jenny lifted her anguished face. 'He's fine Sue, he's fine. He's a lovely little boy. But I just thought that he might have been hit by that car and he might have been hurt and it was so real that…that, Sue, I couldn't stand it.'

Fortunately Sue was a nurse, she could guess what Jenny was going through. And she was a mother, too. So she knelt by the wheelchair, spread her arms around both Sam and Jenny. 'We'll all be well soon,' she whispered.

And slowly the stress passed.

'It's interesting how we've changed,' Mike said, three weeks after she'd moved into the house. 'When you moved in I used to worry all the time about how you'd manage. All I could think was that you'd had an accident, you were an invalid, I had to be careful not to make things worse. But now you're you again. I see you, not someone who's been hurt.'

'Good. And you've stopped treating me as if I might break every time you touch me. So we move on to the next step. I want to go back to work.'

'You can't! Don't even think of it!'

'I can. And I've thought of it quite a lot. I can lecture, I can see students, I can even do a bit of work on the wards. And don't forget the new rules. The department is wheelchair friendly.'

'But you're—'

'I'm capable of work. And, Mike, I'm bored out of my skull!'

'Even with the delights of my constant companionship?'

'Even then. And there's another thing. I know Sue's been invited to go away to visit an old friend and take Sam. She won't go while she thinks I'm still an invalid. If I'm working she'll know that I'm getting back to normal.'

He nodded. 'I'll tell her that she should go. I can look after you.'

'Mike! I don't need looking after, I just want to go back to work. I'm going to phone the boss tomorrow morning.'

He looked thoughtful. 'Let me have a word with him first. I'll get him to come round and talk to you. I must say, he's been having quite a time of it without you. Says he never quite realised just how much you did for him.'

'Nice to be appreciated,' said Jenny. 'Now, practicalities. I'll go in with you when it's convenient for you—and only then. The rest of the time I'll travel by taxi.'

She should have known that that would start a further argument.

It was arranged that she was to start on a Friday, just to see how things went. She was to work for only half a day. Then there would be the weekend off. If things went well, she was to come in only for half a day at a time, and only when she felt up to it. Her own consultant had phoned Mr Spenser who had said that a limited work schedule could do her nothing but good. But it must be limited. And the university medical department was overjoyed.

Going back was odd. Her room—her very own room—seemed strange. Many people stopped her to say how pleased they were to see her. Of course, all her friends had been round to see her but seeing them again as colleagues was odd. And if she saw pity in two or three faces, she tried to ignore it.

She was scheduled to give a lecture. She felt strangely nervous, though there was no need, she had prepared and delivered the same lecture often before. But she wasn't sure how she would feel as she bumped her way into the lecture theatre, her notes on her lap.

She wasn't expecting it but when she entered, her class stood and clapped. And that was a shock. For a moment emotion took over, she thought she could almost feel the goodwill of the group. Her chest constricted, she felt tears prick her eyes and she wondered if she'd be able to get one sensible sentence out. But then she swallowed, fought back. She was Jenny Carson, midwife and lecturer, a professional. She didn't give way to unnecessary shows of feeling.

'Thank you all. And before any of you ask, I'm feeling fine. I'd also like to thank you all for the flowers you sent, the presents, the visits and the messages of goodwill. But now it's time to work. We will talk about the care of the baby who just doesn't seem to be gaining weight...'

It was good to be back in harness. Her back ached a little, but that was all. She could cope with it. Mike took time off at lunchtime to drive her home—as he had driven her in that morning. Sue had gone on her visit with Sam, and this would be the first time Jenny had been alone in the house. 'I'll be all right,' she insisted to Mike. 'All right, yes, I will keep my mobile with me at all times. And I'll phone you if there's any trouble.'

She grinned to herself as he left, wondered how long it would be before he phoned her to make sure all was well.

Then she wheeled herself into the kitchen and prepared a meal. She was tired of being useless.

They were alone in the house that evening. There was a peculiar intimacy as she and Mike sat at the kitchen table and ate their evening meal.

Like any other long-established couple, in the evening they sat together on the couch and watched television. His arm was round her shoulder and from time to time he kissed her, gently, tenderly. And soon it was time for bed.

He kissed her again, in the same relaxed way. But this time she put her arms around his neck, pulled him to her, kissed him properly. She felt the muscles of his arms and chest tense in surprise. Then he gently eased her away.

'What's the matter?' she asked. 'Don't you love me any more?'

He looked at her, wide-eyed. 'Of course I love you!'

'Do you like making love to me?'

'How can you ask that? I can't tell you how much I miss it. I miss being with you that way so desperately. But I've got you with me and that's all that matters.'

Her voice was firm, she was proud of it. 'I want you to make love to me tonight.'

'But Jenny, how can we—?'

'We can with a little bit of thought. My scars have healed, the stitches are long gone. My legs may be paralysed but a lot of the rest of me still has feelings. And if you're really worried, I'll tell you that I phoned Mr Spenser this afternoon. He said that things should be fine.'

Mike blinked. 'Jenny, I don't know what to—'

'I'm going to wash now and then go to bed. And I want you to come to me when I call. That all right?'

She wriggled herself into her wheelchair and was gone before he could answer.

It was a warm night. She washed and then eased herself into bed. She was practised now, it was easy.

The only covering she needed was a sheet. She pulled it up to her chin, switched off all the lights but the bedside light. Then she called to him.

He came into the room, and with an abandon that she hadn't known she possessed, she pulled aside the sheet. She wanted to be naked before him. 'Now you undress,' she said.

She watched the shadowy form moving, heard the rustle of clothes and then he, too, was naked. He came to her. 'I'm still afraid of hurting you,' he said, his voice thick.

'You can't hurt me, you love me. Do you know how much I've missed having you...with me?'

'As much as I've missed you,' he growled.

'Well, you can start by kissing me. And not as if you're kissing your grandmother.'

There was a change in the tone of his voice, a slight edge of humour. 'This won't be like kissing my grandmother. I can promise you that.'

He bent over her, his lips touched hers. She put her arms around him, tried to pull him down onto her. He resisted. In a mocking voice he said, 'If I'm going to kiss you, I want to do it in my own way.'

She wondered what he meant. But what he was doing was pretty good.

First he kissed her lips, her face. Then he trailed kisses down her neck and her throat and she clutched him to her as she realised what he was going to do. He kissed her breasts, holding the pinkness between his lips until she ached with need for him. 'Mike...please, Mike, now...Mike, I need you, come to me.'

But it was no good, he had his own ideas. He ran his tongue over the gentle swell of her belly and then further below. 'Mike, please… You mustn't… Oh, Mike…'

She sighed, then panted with ecstasy as his tongue found places where there was so much pleasure, so much joy that she thought she might die of rapture. And finally there was that explosion that went on and on, that sensation that made her scream his name and smash her arms into the bedding.

Then he crouched beside her head, put his cheek next to hers. For a while she was content just to lie there. Then she whispered, 'Mike, I'm ready now. I promise to tell you if it hurts but you must try. Please, Mike, you've given me so much, I want to share it.'

He paused. Then with infinite delicacy he knelt astride her on her narrow bed. She ran her hands over his body, could feel his urgency, his need for her. A great happiness came to her, this is what she wanted to do. Not for him, for them.

Gently he lowered himself onto her, into her. And it was fine. It felt like coming home. Shortly afterwards she knew he had shared in what she had just felt. 'I love you so much,' she whispered.

'I don't want to leave you. I won't leave you, but you go to sleep.'

She heard him leave the room and two minutes later he came back carrying a pillow and a sheet. He lay on the floor by the side of her bed. He reached up and took her hand. And they both slept.

\* \* \*

She was back at work on Monday, feeling just fine. There was a great backlog of work for her to do so she sat in her office and ploughed her way through. Assessments to be made, essays to be marked, a spreadsheet for next year's programme to be compiled.

And she knew that Mike was busy, too, so she told him that he was to stop thinking that he had to look after her. 'If I need you, I can bleep you. And I will. But for now you're not to worry about me.'

'I shall worry if I want. But it's not worry, it's concern—and love.'

'Whatever. Mike, life is better for me if I work.'

It was one of the rare occasions that she let her guard drop, let him know that underneath the tough exterior she had decided to adopt she was terrified. And he recognised her fear and showed her that he shared it. 'I guess it's better for me, too. I…think about you a lot.'

They could still work together. She was showing two of her midwife students round the postnatal ward, chatting to the mothers, looking at—and admiring—the babies, pointing out to the trainees what they would have to look out for when they worked here.

Mike was on the ward with Maria Wyatt, one of the newly graduated midwives. He gave Jenny a casual wave and a wink. 'Come and say hello to Mrs Elkins,' he said, 'and bring your young ladies with you. Mrs Elkins would like a chat.'

Jenny recognised the signs. Most mothers were willing to let students observe or examine them, they recognised it as a necessary part of medical education. And there were some—Mrs Elkins?—who loved to be on display.

So she, Mike and the two students went to stand by the curtained bed while Maria made her escape. They were introduced to a beaming Mrs Elkins. 'It's me breasts,' she said. 'Do you want to see?' She pulled her nightie back from her shoulders.

'Mrs Elkins gave birth yesterday,' Mike said, somehow managing to keep a straight face. 'She has a slight temperature and complains that her breasts have swollen. They're hard and tender. Miss Carson, would you like to take over now?'

Jenny nodded. 'What are the possible causes?' she asked her two charges.

'Mastitis?' offered one.

'Certainly a possibility. How could you be sure it was mastitis?'

'There should be a reddened section of the breast,' said the other girl, 'and it should be even more tender.'

'Good. Can you find this reddened section?'

After a particularly careful scrutiny, no reddened section was found.

'What's another diagnosis?' Jenny asked.

'Simple breast engorgement. Wear a good maternity bra, bathe the breasts in warm water, lower liquid intake.'

'Excellent. Do we suppress lactation?'

'No.' The girl speaking smiled at Mrs Elkins and said, 'you do want to breastfeed, don't you? Did you have a little boy or a girl?'

'A little girl, Evie. And I was breastfed and she will be, too.'

'I was guilty there,' Jenny said when she was talking afterwards to her two trainee midwives. 'Just for a moment I forgot that I was dealing with a person, not a case. Your questions about breastfeeding and the name were very necessary. You made it personal. You both did well, you know your theory perfectly. More importantly, you know how to deal with people.' She grinned. 'Theory's fine. But it's different when you're faced with a real breast.'

It was Thursday evening and Jenny thought she could at last see an end to the paperwork she had to do. She had told people that working half-days didn't suit her, and from now on she would work full-time. And so now she was both tired and pleased.

'We're going somewhere different,' Mike told her when he picked her up at the end of the working day. 'Sue knows. She's going to wait tea for us.'

'Where are we going?'

'It's a little surprise. Life is more exciting if you get a surprise occasionally.'

You are telling me, she thought, but said nothing.

They drove back near her old flat, it gave her an odd thrill to pass it. Mike had been there quite regularly to fetch stuff for her, but she had not been there since her accident.

'You like it around here, don't you?' he asked.

'Very much so. I like being near the sea, I like being able to see it even if I have to stand on a stool.'

He laughed. 'Me, too. So you'll like…'

He drove into the forecourt of a block of flats, a more expensive-looking block than the one she occupied. And a block that faced the sea. He parked, fetched her wheelchair from the back of his car and placed it by her door. 'You're on your own now,' he told her. 'I'm just going to tag along behind.' He dropped a set of keys into her lap. 'There's the front door.'

He wouldn't say any more, so she wheeled herself to the door he had indicated and managed to let herself in. Rather a more luxurious foyer than the one in her block. And there was a lift as well as stairs.

'Top floor,' said Mike.

So she wheeled herself into the lift, pressed the button for the top floor. There she left the lift. There were two doors opening off the landing. 'That one,' said Mike.

'Mike, what is all this? It's nice to go visiting but I've had a hard day and I'm hungry.'

His expression was imperturbable. 'All will be revealed. You've got the key. Let yourself in.'

So she did, and wheeled herself into the living room. It was a pleasant room. Some furniture, not too much, again quite pleasant. But that didn't make the room. What did was the windows. There were windows on two sides, one leading out onto a balcony. And from them both there was a fantastic view of the river. She moved forward, wanting to see what she could. A panoramic view, the channel of the river, lights from not too distant towns and the grey peaks of the Welsh hills. She could sit and look at this view for ever.

Mike saw her fascination, left her to gaze for a while. Then he said, 'See what you think of the other rooms.'

She could get into them all. There were two bedrooms, a further small room that could be used as a bedroom or a study. 'Like it?' he asked. 'Like to live here?'

'I'd love to live here, you know that. But I want to know what your interest is.'

He looked at her with the quizzical, assessing look she had seen before. 'I've leased this place for a year. At the end of that time I have the option to buy. The flat, not the furniture. I can move in as soon as I like. Harry will be back soon and, though I know the pair of them will be happy for both of us to stay as long as we like, I want a place of my own.'

'I think that's a good idea,' she said. She had no idea where this conversation was going.

'I've had a chat with the rehabilitation people— the ones who got you to exercise and so on. They say that even if you…you have to stay in the wheelchair for only six months, the sooner you learn to look after yourself the better. Like I said, Sue would have you for ever but I thought that…'

'I love living with Sue and Sam—and you, of course—but I do want to be independent,' she said. 'But there's no way I could afford somewhere like this. Though I'd like to.'

'I don't want to push you into anything. My suggestion is…I've leased this place. Your place has no lift, you can't live there. So why don't you move in with me?'

She hadn't expected that. At first the idea seemed very attractive. They would be living together. She would like that. But then… No. She had made up her mind that she wouldn't enter into any kind of long-term relationship with Mike until she was well. Then they could decide.

She shook her head. 'It's lovely of you to offer, Mike,' she said. 'But I just can't. I'd get used to being with you. I'd want to stay, whatever happened to me.'

'I want you to stay! When you're finally cured, when you can walk again…'

'Mike! The word you are looking for is *if* I can walk again.'

There was a silence. 'All right. *If* you can walk again. But the offer is the same. Jenny, after the accident you and everyone else told me not to feel guilty. So I didn't. But helping you in this way will make me feel better. I'll be giving something back.'

'Is that the only reason?'

'No. I want to do it because there's nothing I want to do in my life but help you. I want you to move in here.'

She wheeled herself to the window, gazed out at the river. She knew she could sit here, watch for ever. 'I just daren't do it,' she said. 'I'm sorry, Mike, but I won't move in with you.'

She knew he was upset but he tried to hide it. 'All right,' he said after a while. 'Then I've got another idea. You move in here. I'll move into your flat.'

'But my flat isn't worth anything like what this one must cost! You'd be…'

He held up his hand. 'Jenny! Don't even think about it! The last thing we two need is to argue about money. For us it just doesn't signify. I'm happy just swapping homes.' He grinned. 'Besides, I expect to be spending a lot of my time here.'

So she thought, and she realised that it wasn't a bad idea. But the thought of the extra money he was paying worried her.

'I'd want to give you something towards the lease here,' she said. 'There's no reason why—'

'Answer me one question, and be honest. If things were the other way round, if I'd been paralysed and you had leased this flat and offered it to me—would you ask or expect extra money from me?'

She thought. 'I suppose not,' she said reluctantly.

'Point made. I have your flat, you have this one.' He grinned. 'I'll even do some decorating for you.'

'No, you won't! I pick my own wallpaper. All right, we'll swap flats. But it's clearly understood. This arrangement is only until one month after Mr Spenser gives me the final verdict. Whatever the result. Right?'

'Right. I hope things will be different by then anyway.'

She wondered exactly what he meant by that.

# CHAPTER SEVEN

'YOU'VE been in my flat a month now,' Mike said. 'You're back to normal. You're the girl I first fell for when I saw you at the party.'

'I'm in a wheelchair,' Jenny pointed out.

'I don't notice that at all now. We're just like your average couple.'

'I suppose you get used to anything.'

She had amazed herself at the range of things she found she was able to do. She had cooked the evening meal, she could wash easily, clean her flat, manage both her job and her shopping. Not being able to drive was the worst thing. But she managed.

'But I am surprised at what I can do,' she added. 'I can do all sorts of things.'

'I know,' he said with a grin. 'But you do need someone with you to help you do them. What would you have done without a double bed?'

'Don't make me blush!'

'I'm just feeling happy,' he said.

It was dark but they were sitting out on the balcony, watching the ships move up the channel. It wouldn't be long now until winter. It was getting chilly and she'd fetched herself a coat. But it was a joy to sit here with him, drink the coffee he'd just made and be quietly comfortable.

They had worked out a routine between them. She

refused to have him there all the time. 'You've got a new job, you often have to work awkward shifts, you need time to yourself. And I want—I need to be independent. I've got a life of my own which is important to me.'

'But I want to share that life.'

'Not all of it you don't. And I don't intend to share it with you. I need some space to myself.'

'Rejected again,' he said glumly. 'My life story.'

But she did spend a lot of time with him and she loved it. And she was getting to know him better. So later, when he asked her, elaborately casually, what she was doing on Saturday night, she knew he had some plan.

'I was hoping to spend some time with you,' she said. 'Why?'

'I thought we might have an evening out. Go back to that place up on the moors we went to last time and have dinner. You haven't had a chance to dress up for a while.'

'Look what happened to me the last time I went there. I woke up next morning with a man in bed with me.'

'Something quite similar happened to me,' he said. 'But you will take the risk and come, won't you?'

'I'd love a dressed-up evening out,' she said.

So it was arranged. But when she lay in bed that night she frowned. She knew there were decisions to be made. And she had to make them in advance.

The following afternoon Jenny felt that she needed something to cheer her up a little so she phoned Sue and asked her if she could go shopping that evening. 'I feel like a little retail therapy,' she said. 'We could borrow Mike's car and ask him to babysit Sam.'

'What a great idea! He's had you to himself far too much recently. Bring him here with you, I'll fix a lightning tea and we'll get straight off.'

'Good. And, Sue, how's the baby coming along?'

'Growing and thriving. I'm beginning to feel really excited, started thinking about names. And Harry'll be home soon. He's going to get a shock.'

'He'll be happy. I'll see you later.' Jenny rang off. She felt better.

'I want yet another party dress,' she told Sue as they parked outside the largest department store. 'Mike's taking me out on Saturday night, I want something a bit special.'

'Another one? Making your total of evening dresses a stunning two? You are being extravagant. Now, what's going on in here?'

They were moving across the ground floor, making their way to the lifts to the third floor where the women's fashions were kept. But there seemed to be some kind of show in front of them. A crowd of women—mostly young—were peering at a small, well-lit stage.

'It's a wedding-dress display,' said Jenny. 'Look, there's a sign advertising it.'

'Let's have a look,' said Sue. 'We've got plenty of time and it's not often I get the chance to get out shopping with another woman. We'll have a laugh for fifteen minutes. Come on.'

'All right,' said Jenny. She had found that most big shops went out of their way to make sure disabled customers were welcome. And most customers were only too happy to make way for her. So it was easy for her and Sue to make their way to the front of the crowd, to sit and watch assorted models come on in assorted wedding dresses.

'Not real models,' Sue whispered after a while. 'They're all smiling.'

'You have to smile in a wedding dress. Part of the contract. Does this bring it all back?'

'And how. Getting married was wonderful. The day was fantastic. And I loved Harry so much. But before, all those decisions! Church, invitations, flowers, dress, reception—there were times when I wondered if it was all worthwhile. I wanted someone just to make it happen.'

'Sounds a good idea.'

Both looked as a creation in pink and yellow appeared in front of them. 'Now, could you walk down the aisle in that?' Sue asked.

'No. No man is worth being seen in that.'

It was an interesting show, fun to sit there and whisper comments to each other. And then, right at the end, came *the* dress. It was simple, a classic long dress in white satin with no ornament at all. There was a lace cap and veil.

'Now, that is absolutely gorgeous,' said Jenny. 'That dress is worth getting married for.'

'Provided you have the right size and figure,' Sue said critically. 'You've got the right bust for it. But, yes, it is gorgeous.'

The show was soon over and it was time for serious shopping.

'I want a trouser suit in linen or some other soft fabric,' Jenny said. 'Perhaps with short sleeves.'

Sue ran her finger down Jenny's arm. 'You should show your arms,' she said. 'All this pulling yourself in and out of the wheelchair is getting you beautifully curved there.'

Jenny grinned. 'And my bust that you mentioned is up half an inch,' she said. 'Because I'm developing big pectorals.'

They had a lovely time shopping. They moved from shop to shop, tried on half a dozen outfits. When they were exhausted they went down to a coffee-shop and had an evil cream cake and coffee. Sue looked at Jenny. 'The lemon one with the low neckline or the blue one with the mandarin collar?'

'The lemon one,' said Jenny.

Once it was said there was no need to think further. They went back upstairs, bought it and drove home happily. 'A job well done,' said Sue. 'There are some things that a man just can't do.'

That night in bed Jenny thought about her new dress. She was looking forward to wearing it on her evening out with Mike. And then she thought about their relationship.

She knew that usually things developed at their own pace. There was the initial meeting, some liking, a gradual getting together and then, almost unnoticed, love. And love grew.

She and Mike had got together very quickly. At

times she still had difficulty in remembering much about it. And then they had decided to take things easy a bit, to get to know each other better, to enjoy the process of finding out about each other.

That plan had been ruined by her accident. The accident had pushed them together in a way that both of them realised was not ideal, and—wisely she thought—they had decided to wait until she was better before making any big plans.

Had they decided that? Or had *she* decided it?

She knew what he was like, he was a man who saw no point in waiting. He was an honourable man, he had done as she'd asked and not pressed her when she'd still been suffering the after-effects of her accident. But now he thought she was better. She was capable of making decisions.

She also realised that he wanted this coming Saturday evening to be something special, something that she would remember. So she needed to be prepared, to think in advance. He was going to ask her to marry him.

Jenny shivered. She loved him so much. But she knew she was going to hurt him.

# CHAPTER EIGHT

THE evening got off to a good start. Jenny had gone to Sue's for the afternoon, to talk to her and to play with Sam. She bathed and changed there. Mike had been doing an extra session at the hospital, he came home and changed. Jenny was in the bathroom when he arrived.

When she wheeled herself out of what used to be her bedroom, in her new lemon dress, she was thrilled to see the look on his face. There was love there, surprise and—when he looked at her rather low-cut front—just a little lust, too. Good. She was wearing the green medallion he had given her, and it rested on the swell of her breasts.

'You look fabulous,' he said, the glazed expression of his eyes showing that he meant every word.

'Thank you. You don't look bad yourself. Did you buy a new suit?'

He held his arms out, pirouetted. 'I can't be entirely outdone by my gorgeous partner,' he said.

He was wearing a light grey mohair suit. It was superbly cut, emphasised his slim waist, the depth of his chest. For once he was conventional in a white silk shirt and a sober burgundy tie. He looked glorious.

'You two enjoy yourselves,' said Sue, kissing

them both. 'Jenny, you're to phone me tomorrow and tell me all about it.'

'I certainly will,' said Jenny. She hoped her confident voice hid her doubts. She was also going to enjoy this evening. She was going to ensure that Mike enjoyed this evening. And things went well. When he'd booked Mike must have told them that she was in a wheelchair as there was a parking place reserved for them right by the front door. The *maître d'hôtel* came to supervise them personally, ensuring that she had an easy passage to their reserved seats in the little lounge. The lady who came to take their coats whispered to Jenny that she had nursing training so if Jenny needed any assistance when going to the cloakroom she would be very happy to help.

The meal was as good as the service. This time Jenny was determined to remember what she had—in fact, she asked if she could take away a menu.

'It will be our pleasure to provide one,' said the *maître d'hôtel*.

As they sat in the lounge they were given a tiny tray of bonnes bouches—fragments of hot pastry with a variety of fillings. Then they were invited into the dining room—seats near the window this time, with views over the moors.

There was so much to choose from. Eventually Jenny chose duck—the restaurant was famous for it. Mike asked for sole.

'Remember the last time we came here?' Mike asked.

'I remember it well. The meal was fantastic. But I was unsure. I knew I liked you a lot—but I hardly knew you and I was a bit frightened. I'd got the wine and so on back at my flat—but only at the last minute did I manage to get the courage together to invite you in.'

'Didn't you know what you wanted?'

'I thought that perhaps I knew what I wanted. Does that make sense?'

'Not a lot,' he said cheerfully, and they both laughed.

'Anyway, this time I can tell you in advance. I've got the same bottles of wine waiting at my flat. I've even got the same party platter that I bought last time.'

'You're just an old romantic,' he said. 'What's my chance of staying the night?'

'As they used to say—you might get lucky, boy.'

And then their first courses arrived.

For the rest of the meal they talked easily, casually, going over the hospital gossip, Mike's plans for the future and what she might do with her course at the university. They talked about their early lives—and once again Jenny wished that she could have had a brother or sister. And then it was time to go.

It was dark now. They swept down the hill, seeing the array of lights below on the Lancashire plain. 'It's quite early, no need to go straight back home,' Mike said. 'Shall we go for a little drive?' His voice was elaborately casual.

'I'd like that,' she said. She made her voice happy, she owed him that.

They drove to the coast down a little road and parked by the beach. It was lonely. There were no lights but the distant Christmas-tree effect of an oil well far out to sea. There were the stars. The tide was in, they could hear the faint noise of the waves.

They sat in silence for a moment. Then he kissed her. And she knew she had to take the initiative, he mustn't start first.

Her voice was urgent. 'Mike, hold my hands, hold both of them tight. Please!'

He did as she'd asked, then said anxiously, 'Sweetheart, are you all right? You sound a bit...unsteady. You're not in any pain or anything?'

His concern hurt her even more, but she had to carry on now she had started. 'Mike, please, listen and try to understand. I know you want to talk but there's something I want to ask you first.'

'You've lost me,' he muttered.

'I want you to listen to me then it'll be your turn. This might be forward of me but I've got to say it. Mike, I love you. I can't imagine loving anyone else, imagine loving you more. I love you.'

'And I love you, sweetheart,' he said urgently. 'I love you so much that I—'

'Mike, please, stop!' Her voice was high as she interrupted him. 'I'm not sure what you were going to say, and this might be even more forward of me.' She stopped and swallowed, made sure her voice was clear. 'I don't want you to ask me to marry you.'

The silence in the car was deafening. Then he said the one thing that might have made her change her mind. Almost like a little boy he said, 'But I love you so much.'

She felt the tears on her face. 'And I love you, too. But I can't…won't marry you.'

'Why not? If we love each other so much, what can stop us?'

'Me being in a wheelchair can stop us.'

'No…it…can…not.'

She had to explain. 'I think I know what you're going to say, that me being in a wheelchair doesn't matter, you love me anyway. And, Mike, I believe you. But I'd feel happier if you'd ask me when…when everything is settled. When we know for certain whether I can…whether I'll ever walk properly again.'

Now he was angry. 'Whether you walk again or not, I don't care. I love you, whatever. You're wrong to think I might change my mind. What do you take me for?'

Desperately she squeezed his hand. 'Please, don't shout, Mike, this is hard enough anyway. And I take you for the man who loves me as much as I love him. I don't think it's much to ask. Wait another three months or so and then we'll know. Ask me then. If you still want to. After all, we've not known each other too long.'

Then there was silence. After a while he took out a little box. He said, 'I was in a bit of a hurry, I didn't have time to buy a ring. So I asked Sue. She lent me this, it was my great-grandmother's ring. I thought you might like to wear it till we got something with diamonds or something.'

He switched on the car's indoor light. Then he opened the box, took out the ring and gave it to her.

It was worn but beautiful, a thing of filigree surrounding an amethyst.

Jenny looked at it. The urge to put it on her finger was almost too much to bear. But she didn't. Instead, she handed it back to him.

'No, Mike. Wait till we know, then we can be certain. You know how much I love you. Please, don't make me say no to you again.'

She heard him breathe out, and by her side his body relaxed. She hadn't realised just how tense he had been or that she had felt his tenseness. But now it seemed to have gone. He leaned over, kissed her gently on the lips. 'I feel a certain sense of anticlimax,' he said. 'This is not the way I expected the evening to end.'

'Mike, I've had a wonderful time. Look, now we know we love each other. We've said so. That's a big step. And now you can take me home. The evening's not over, you know. And what did you say about climax?'

He shook his head. 'You're just too much,' he said. He started the car, and then stopped it. 'You've just turned me down, you know. And I'll do what you say, I won't ask you again. But I'm going to be pushing you. You know me, I don't like noes.'

She sighed. 'I'll give you the same answer. But I love you for asking.'

And then he drove off.

Their love-making that night was different. There was a sense of desperation about him. But finally, after calling his name in that ecstatic way that she always did, as she collapsed into his arms, he gasped that he loved her.

'And I love you, too, sweetheart,' she murmured, 'more than you can guess.' So perhaps things would be all right.

She fell asleep soon after that. Mike lay still, but awake, listening to her heavy breathing. Her hand was curled in his. Usually he slept at once but tonight was different. He couldn't get her answer out of his mind.

She wouldn't agree to marry him and he was disappointed. But he had to respect her honesty. She hadn't said no, she just didn't want to be asked yet. Until they knew exactly what her future was. Then he could ask her. And she had indicated that she would say yes.

Well, that was good but he was a man in a hurry. Certainly he'd wait as long as she liked for the actual ceremony. But he wanted her to say yes. To say yes now. He would ask her to marry him whether she was in a wheelchair or not. He didn't want her thinking that he was waiting to see if she'd recover or not.

Then something struck him. He had seen her toughness. Perhaps if she found out that she would have to stay in a wheelchair for the rest of her life, she'd refuse to marry him. Out of consideration for him!

The idea was so possible—and so unpleasant—that for a moment he was tempted to wake her, to ask her to marry him there and then. Then he smiled sourly as he remembered. Jenny was never at her best when first woken up, she'd most probably turn him down.

She had to marry him! But he'd be careful how in his approach. She had a mind of her own.

Jenny was alone when Sue rang her next morning. She and Mike had just finished a late breakfast and he had gone to her flat to change his clothes so Jenny and Sue could talk without anyone overhearing.

Sue often phoned just for a chat, but this time Jenny guessed that it was more than that. She decided to tell her friend what had happened. 'Did you know he was going to ask me to marry him?' she asked Sue.

Sue was thrown by this question. 'Well, I wondered when he asked to borrow that ring,' she said after a while. 'But, Jenny, you did say yes, didn't you? I would so much like—'

'I asked him not to ask me,' said Jenny.

'What?'

Jenny found it hard not to laugh at her friend's amazement. She tried to explain and felt that at the end Sue understood.

'But you know that he won't accept that, don't you?' Sue said. 'He's tough when he gets his teeth into something. He'll be nice and he'll keep any promise he's made, but he'll keep pushing somehow.'

Jenny sighed. 'You can't guess just how worried I am about all this,' she said. 'But I still feel I'm right. And…and…I hope everything comes out well between us.'

She knew that Sue had detected the tremor in her voice. And her friend said briskly, 'It'll come out well, don't worry. But it might not be the way you expect. Now, can I tell you my good news?'

Jenny had thought that Sue seemed even more full of life than usual. 'Go on,' she said.

'Just heard this morning. Harry's on his way home. He should be here in another week or so.'

'Sue, that's wonderful! You know I'm so much looking forward to meeting him.'

'So am I,' said Sue.

Mike came back shortly afterwards. Without saying anything, they both seemed to agree that this was not the time for further emotion. And it was pouring with rain. So they sat together, read, had a simple tea, watched TV and went to bed early.

'I like the simple life with you,' he said.

She knew he meant it. But she wondered how much longer her life would remain simple.

Next day Mike was working away from the hospital at a clinic, but he drove Jenny in and dropped her off. She would take a taxi home. Jenny was almost glad to find that she had a pile of paperwork needing her attention. In work she could find a respite from her churning emotions.

There were reports on her third-year students and Jenny reached for the one on Ann Mallon. There were varied comments by people Ann had worked for, including an account of a big mistake she had made some months ago.

Ann, it seemed, had been working in the antenatal

ward. She had accompanied a patient down to the delivery suite as the birth seemed imminent. All seemed to be going well.

All the student midwives were told how important it was to maintain a comforting presence with the mothers, to chat to them and try to keep them from becoming too nervous. Ann had done this. But she had not noticed how pale and sweaty the mother had become. She hadn't quite got round to checking the now high blood pressure or the too rapid pulse. Only when she had felt the woman's abdomen, discovered how hard it was, had she wondered if something might be wrong.

And at the moment an experienced midwife had come into the room, realised what was wrong and had instantly buzzed for help. The woman had been in shock. She had an ante-partum haemorrhage, the baby was in danger of drowning in its own blood.

Fortunately it hadn't been too late. The emergency had been controlled and the baby delivered safely. But what little confidence Ann had seemed to have disappeared. Jenny could almost sympathise.

Jenny rang the sister in antenatal to enquire how Ann was doing.

'Ann? She's very willing,' said the sister. 'She'll do anything I ask her. What she won't do is what I don't ask her. She never uses her initiative, she's frightened that she's made a mistake in even the simplest of observations. She repeats them over and over, and the mums tend to get a bit annoyed with her. Which makes her worse. And she keeps running to me to ask me to check what she's doing.'

'Is there anything at all she's good at? Any way we could praise her?'

There was a moment's silence. 'It's not too much, but there is one thing. She's formed quite a good relationship with one of the mums. Apparently they went to the same school, knew each other vaguely. The mum's in long time with placenta praevia grade four. We're watching her for a bleed. She used to be a trouble to us, now Ann has quietened her down, made her much more happy. More ready to rest. And that's been very useful.'

'It's a start,' said Jenny. 'If it's all right with you, I'll come onto the ward and have a word with her. Tell her she's doing well with this case and can she do the same for any of the other mums?'

'Worth a try. We're short of midwives. So I'll see you later?'

'Don't tell Ann that I'm coming,' said Jenny.

She replaced the phone and thought about the girl. As tutor it was part of her job to try to bring the best out in each of her students, to make sure they passed. But she also had a duty to make sure that no one got a qualification to be a midwife unless they deserved it.

Jenny decided she'd have to see more of Ann. But there was hope.

By the middle of the afternoon her back was starting to ache. It did sometimes, usually when she had spent too long sitting at her desk. Almost automatically her hands went to the arms of her wheelchair.

Then she realised what she had been about to do.

Stand up on tiptoe, reach her arms up into the air.
Stretch her cramped muscles and make the blood
flow again. It was what she used to do when she had
been studying for too long. But now she couldn't.
Her legs were paralysed. Her previously broken arm
was still weak.

It wasn't a feeling she was proud of, but suddenly
Jenny felt very sorry for herself.

Someone knocked on her door. Jenny sighed, she
could have done with a few more minutes without
company. But, still, whoever it was might take her
mind off her miseries. 'Come in,' she shouted.

'Jenny Carson?' A tall sunburned man with tired
eyes came through the door. For a moment Jenny
remembered how sunburned Mike had been when
she'd first met him. And Mike was tall... What was
she thinking of?

'Yes, that's me,' she said. 'May I help you?'

'I think you already have. More than I can thank
you for. I'm Harry Morris. I'm Sue's husband and
Sam's dad.'

'You're not expected until the end of the week!'

He laughed. 'I got home early. In fact, I arrived
late last night.'

'I'm sorry, that was a stupid thing to say. Please,
come in. I was just going to have a coffee. Do you
want one? If you're looking for Mike, I'm afraid he's
away at a clinic. And have a seat.'

Jenny was aware she was rambling, but Harry's
arrival had been the last thing she had been expecting.

Harry sat, said he'd like a black coffee. 'It doesn't

matter about Mike, I'll catch up with him later. I'm still a bit jet-lagged, we'll probably have a long session when I feel more myself.'

He paused and looked at Jenny. 'In fact, I came to see you. Sue told me about the accident to you and Sam only this morning. It came as a bit of a shock, and then I learned that I was going to be a father a second time. Twice in our married life she's kept something from me.' Then his face softened. 'What am I saying? I know she did it for me. And Sam is perfectly all right.'

'He's a lovely little boy,' said Jenny.

'He is. You saved his life. And because of that you're in a wheelchair.'

It was easy to see that Harry was a soldier. He had a military way of bearing himself, his face remained calm, his voice tended to be clipped. He obviously didn't like to show emotion. But as he spoke Jenny could tell how deeply he felt.

'Look, I was there,' she said. 'I would have done the same for any child. And I've got rather fond of Sam.'

He nodded. 'But you've still been hurt. When Sue told me this morning I knew I had to come to see you at once to thank you. If ever there's any way I can help you, any way at all—please, ask.'

'I will,' she said.

For a moment both drank their coffee. Then Harry said, 'I hear you're getting to know my brother-in-law quite well.'

It took Jenny a moment to realise that he meant Mike. 'I think the accepted expression these days is

that we're an item,' she said. 'I like him quite a lot.'
Then she went slightly red under Harry's steady scrutiny.

'I'm indebted to him, too,' Harry said. 'He introduced me to Sue. You know we are good friends from way back? We were at medical school together, climbed together in the Lake District.'

Jenny was interested, she hadn't realised that. 'What was he like as a young man?'

Harry laughed. 'Much the same as he is today, I suspect. He sees what he wants and goes for it. And he likes to cut corners—got into trouble for that at medical school. Said he was there to learn how to look after the sick, not fill in forms.'

Jenny nodded. 'He still hates unnecessary paperwork.'

'As students we had to take it in turns to organise seminars. Introduce a subject and then discuss it. We'd sit in the commonroom, drink coffee and carry on for hours. When it was Mike's turn to lead the seminar he made us all stand in the middle of the room. Said he believed that decisions could be made in a quarter of the time if there was no coffee and no sitting down. And he was right.'

Jenny laughed. 'I couldn't imagine working life without coffee.'

'He may have mellowed a bit that way,' said Harry, and stood. 'Now, I'll leave you to your work. I just had to see you after I heard about you and Sam. Be coming to dinner soon, won't you?'

'I'd like that,' said Jenny.

He bent, kissed her gently on the cheek. 'I know

Sue's said it, but I'll say it, too,' he said. 'Welcome to the family. Now I'll be off.'

Jenny sat in silence for a minute when he had gone, and thought. It was rather a convoluted thought. But if she was married to Mike she'd have a sister-in-law who she very much liked—Sue. And now a brother-in-law who she thought she'd like just as much—Harry. A ready-made family. That would be nice.

She was in her office later that afternoon when her phone rang. It was Mike. 'I'm in the consulting room, about to perform a foetal blood sampling,' he said. 'Got a slightly worrying CTG here so I want to check the baby's pH levels. I wondered if you'd like to bring one of your students along. She could watch and you could talk her through what I'm doing. I'll be a bit busy myself.'

'Great idea. I've got a group in the postnatal ward, I'll fetch one.'

And it would mean she could watch Mike at work. She liked that.

Mike had already discussed the situation with the mother before Jenny arrived with her student. He had got the mother's permission for the student to observe. He had explained what he was going to do, told the mother that in no way could her baby be harmed. And he had had the mother placed in the left lateral position.

The mother smiled wanly as Jenny and the student came in. 'Hope you can learn something,' she said.

'He's using an amnioscope with a light source fitted,' Jenny whispered. 'The cervix is now dilated so he can pass it through and actually touch the baby's head.'

She heard Mike grunt with satisfaction, then he waved the student over to him. 'Look through here,' he said. 'Jenny will tell you what you're seeing.'

The student peered, then scampered back to Jenny's side.

'He's going to take a tiny sample of the baby's blood,' Jenny went on. 'He'll clean the scalp and put a touch of silicone jelly on it. That will make sure that the blood forms a globule—which will be easier to collect.'

'Won't the baby start bleeding?'

'There'll be one stab at the scalp with a guarded blade. Then the blood is collected in a collection tube and a swab pressed over the wound. Usually the bleeding stops pretty quickly.'

'And all that done through that tiny tube?'

'You have to have delicate fingers,' said Jenny.

The blood was collected, tested at once. The pH was well within acceptable range, no great need to worry.

Mike told the mother that all was well, turned and winked at Jenny and her student. 'I'll be down to see you in a couple of minutes,' he told Jenny.

Jenny took the hint. She took the student outside, explained again what had happened and then went back to her own room. She was pleased that Mike took his responsibilities as a teacher quite seriously. Too many senior medical staff tended to ignore the needs of student midwives.

                    *     *     *

'A job well done,' Mike said a little later as he accepted a coffee. 'A negative result, which is what we want. It's good to feel competent at your job, isn't it, Sister?'

'It's also good to be modest about it,' she pointed out.

'Very possibly. Now, do you feel relaxed? Feel at peace with the world? Feel in a giving mood?'

She looked at him suspiciously. 'I don't think I do. I think you're plotting, you're about to make demands. Don't you just want to take me home?'

'Later I do, certainly. But yesterday, on the way back from the clinic, I passed that posh little precinct. I thought I'd have a look round. There's a shop just opened that specialises in unit furniture. There was some shelving there that I thought might do for the flat. Other stuff as well. I'd value your advice.'

She was still suspicious. Certainly she had been encouraging him to look around for more furniture for the flat, but why was he interested now? When he adopted this completely innocent expression she wondered if he had some ulterior plan in mind. Still…perhaps she was being unduly sceptical. 'All right, let's go,' she said.

She had been wrong. There was a shop, there was some interesting shelving there and they spent a happy half-hour picking out a style that they liked. They walked out of the shop with a catalogue and a firm intention to work out exactly how much shelving they needed.

He was fiddling with something on his wrist. 'This

watchstrap is breaking,' he mumbled as they moved back to where he'd parked the car. 'I need to get it fixed. Let's see if they'll do it here while we wait.' They were passing a jewellery shop.

So they went inside and he handed over the watch. 'Can you fit me another strap just like that?'

'It'll be ten minutes, sir.'

'May as well look round while we're waiting,' Mike said to her. 'Now, these are engagement rings.'

'Mike Donovan! Of all the two-faced, cheating, brazen…you're the worst! You got me in here to look at engagement rings!'

His face could not have been more innocent. 'Me? Why would I do that? All I need is a watchstrap. But since we're here, let's look.'

She couldn't help it. She wheeled herself nearer the counter, looked at the display he had pointed out.

'Would you say you are a diamond girl? Solitaire or cluster? Or a ruby, or an emerald? I like that one— do you?'

She was hypnotised by them. The bright lights, the dark velvet setting, drew her to them. She knew she was an unusual woman. She'd never been much interested in jewellery. But somehow…these were different.

'That ruby looks good to me,' he murmured.

Well, yes, it did. But… 'It's all right. But I think something green. What about the emerald?'

There were three rings for them to look at, to consider and compare. And then she saw it. It was unusual, a jade heart surrounded by tiny diamonds. And as she looked at it, she knew she wanted it. 'Look at that, Mike! It's absolutely stunning.'

'So it is. And the green would match your eyes, sweetheart. Shall I ask him to get it out so you can try it on? Just to look, of course.'

At that moment the jeweller returned with the new watchstrap. 'Is there anything you'd like to see, madam?'

She had to speak quickly. 'Nothing at all, thank you, and we have to go now. I'll see you outside, Mike.' And she wheeled herself out of the shop.

Mike joined her a minute later. 'That was a bit low,' she said.

He raised his eyebrows. 'Just passing the time,' he said, and waved his wrist at her. 'Got a nice new strap for my watch. Did you like that ring?'

'Yes, I did like that ring. I loved it. And never mind your watchstrap! Mike, let's get one thing straight. If you suddenly turn up with that ring and say let's get engaged, I will be seriously annoyed. And under no circumstance will I ever wear it! Everything is on hold until we're clearer about my condition.'

He was not a man who could easily hide his emotions. She could tell he was upset. 'But you know I still love you,' she said. 'I love you more than anyone or anything I've ever loved. Isn't that enough?'

'More than enough,' he said.

It was time for her visit to see Mr Spenser. She'd seen him last a month ago, then a fortnight before that. 'We'll just see how things go,' he had said. 'Nature and time are the best healers. So we'll give them both a chance. Now, has there been any extension of feeling—any movement at all?'

'Not really,' she had said. And though he had tried to conceal it, she had known that he had been disappointed.

Now Mike wanted to come with her.

'You can drive me there and drive me back, Mike,' she said, 'but things aren't as desperate as the first time I saw him. Then I really needed you. But now I can manage. I think I can manage better than you can. And if I feel you getting upset, that makes me worse.'

She saw the pain on his face but he said, 'I guess I know what you mean. You're good to me, Jenny.'

Before she saw Mr Spenser there were the X-rays, CT and MRI scans, all the aids that science could give him to work out a diagnosis. Then she went to his rooms.

As before, there was a lengthy examination. His eyes flicked from examining her back to the X-rays and other scans which were illuminated on the wall. He prodded at her legs and back, asked her a variety of questions, about her general health, her diet, how she was dealing with work, how she coped with any depression. Then he sat opposite her and stared at her.

'Has there been any progress?' she asked him directly.

Slowly he shook his head. 'Not as much as I had hoped, there's not been enough change. I had hoped that the natural processes might have built up sufficient strength by now but...they haven't. However, you seem to have coped with the…change in your circumstances very well. You've got a positive attitude to life.'

'Not always,' she said, and he nodded.

'You're human, not superhuman,' he said. 'You're entitled to feel sorry for yourself from time to time.'

'So I ought to look forward to a life in a wheelchair?'

'I wouldn't put things quite as starkly as that. We still have some time, things might improve. But…I had hoped…'

He picked up her case notes. 'I'd like your permission to take all the details of your case down to London,' he said. 'There's an American professor coming over for a neurological conference, his area of expertise covers your injury.'

He looked at her over his glasses. 'We're not looking for anything special, you understand. Just that looking at your notes might interest him. Might help us extend the boundaries of medical knowledge a little.'

'I'm happy to do that. Happy to help anyone in the same condition as myself.'

'Good.' Mr Spenser rose, shook her hand. 'Don't forget, any new symptoms, any change at all in your condition, phone my secretary at once. Don't try to get out of the wheelchair. And I'll see you again in a month.'

'Right. Thank you, Mr Spenser.'

It had gone as she'd expected.

*     *     *

Mike was waiting for her outside. He saw her set face, must have recognised her mood. So he bent to kiss her on the cheek and asked, 'No special news?'

'No news at all. Things are as they were before, as we expected. My legs are still paralysed, I'm in a wheelchair, we just have to wait and see if things improve. But they won't.'

He said nothing, just took her hand and held it.

'I don't want to go straight back to my room,' she said, 'to say hello to people and tell them that there's nothing to report. Just for once I'm tired of being brave. Mike, push me over there.'

The hospital grounds were quite extensive. There were large stretches of lawn, occasional thickets of bushes and trees. For once she just didn't want to wheel herself, and kept her hands in her lap as Mike pushed her towards the little stand of trees she had indicated.

There was a bench there, he sat on it and eased her so she was by his side. And when he put an arm around her, her tears started to flow.

'Everyone is so good to me,' she sobbed. 'And then there's you, and I know things could get worse. But sometimes I feel terrified. And I feel alone.'

'You're not alone! Jenny, you've got me.'

'I know that. Without you I couldn't have coped. But I guess I'm frightened. And the nearer I get to having no hope—the more frightened I get.'

'There's no need to be. You know, whatever happens, I will never leave you. And there's always hope.'

'Just hold me,' she said.

So he put his arms round her. She could feel the warmth of his body and it comforted her. After a while she took out a handkerchief, rubbed at her face. 'I'm sorry,' she said. 'I shouldn't get depressed in front of you like this, I know it only upsets you.'

He was indignant. 'Of course you can lean on me! And I can deal with any upset.' Then he went on, 'Of course, you could have a legal right to upset me. I could stand up and promise to look after you—in sickness and in health. Or is this a poor time to bring up the subject?'

She had to smile. 'It is a poor time. But knowing that you want to keeps me warm inside and keeps me alive.'

Then she spoke in a stronger voice. 'We'd better get back. We're both needed at work.'

# CHAPTER NINE

IT WAS time to do something about Ann Mallon. Jenny had called on the ward to see the girl a couple of times, now she asked the ward sister if Ann could come over for a coffee and a talk.

'I think she could be good,' the ward sister said. 'Don't be too hard on her.'

'I won't. I suspect she's too hard on herself.'

Ann knocked on her door five minutes later. At first she was defensive, saying very little. Jenny had decided to be calm with the student, to try and reinforce the good things that she had done. Ann seemed to be suffering from a crippling sense of her own inadequacy.

'I've been thinking about giving up the course,' she said. 'I'll be just no good as a midwife.'

Jenny leafed through the notes on her desk. 'You've passed every exam, every test so far,' she pointed out. 'It seems a pity to get this far and then give it all up. Don't you like the work?'

Ann burst into tears. 'I just can't forget it,' she sobbed. 'I thought I'd got it right at last, I was really enjoying myself, and then, and then...I didn't notice and that woman nearly died.'

'But she didn't,' Jenny said. 'All right, you made a mistake. But we work in a system that means that mistakes can be corrected. That woman now has a beautiful baby, partly thanks to you. Now, you say you were enjoying yourself before it happened?'

'I was. I was happy.'

'Have you felt that way since?'

'Never,' said Ann.

'Let's see if we can do something about that. Come on, we're going to the delivery suite.'

Angela Lamb was in the second stage of labour. All seemed to be going well. This was to be her third child and she seemed as delighted with the prospect as her husband was. This should be a perfect, trouble-free birth.

The midwife in charge was Lucy Stephens. Jenny nodded to herself. Lucy was just the midwife she needed for what he had in mind.

Ann was still a student so the mother's permission had to be asked for her—and for Jenny—to be present. And to assist.

'No problem,' gasped Angela. 'The more the merrier.'

Ann and Jenny were introduced to the father, who was sitting there, holding his wife's hands. He smiled vaguely and Jenny realised he hadn't even realised that she was in a wheelchair.

Angela had opted not to have an epidural, had been pushing for perhaps an hour in time with the contractions. The birth was now imminent.

Jenny wheeled herself well back out of the way. She couldn't count the number of births she had seen but she still felt the magic of this moment, could share in the emotion of the parents. There were tears running down the face of the husband.

But Jenny was here to observe Ann and she saw conflicting emotions. There was fear there certainly, but also delight.

'I can see the head,' Lucy called. 'Not long now, Angela. Keep pushing till I tell you.'

Jenny saw Ann reach up, wipe Angela's face and smile at her encouragingly.

'Right, Angela. Don't push any more. Just pant. The baby's coming, just pant.'

The baby's head was born. From somewhere Ann seemed to have found all the confidence she needed. She cleaned the baby's face, aspirated mucus from nose, mouth and throat. Then she watched as the shoulders rotated.

Angela was asked to push again. Ann drew the baby's head downwards, delivered the anterior shoulder. All straightforward now. Angela was given an injection of Syntometrine after the baby was fully delivered. 'A little girl,' cried Lucy. The cord was clamped.

Lucy let Ann wrap the baby in a warm blanket and hand her to her mother.

Jenny decided that Ann didn't need her any longer. Quietly, she left the room. There was plenty of work for Ann still to do, but Lucy would keep an eye on her and Jenny was confident that she'd do well.

A couple of hours later Ann came to her room. 'Lucy said I did well,' she said.

'I thought you did well. Did you enjoy it?'

'I was nervous at first. Of course, I knew what to do, and I've done it before but…today was special.' Then she said in a stronger voice, 'You took me there to boost my confidence, didn't you?' This was already a new Ann.

Carefully, Jenny said, 'I thought you needed reminding of the skills you have and the pleasure that being a midwife can bring. Still thinking about leaving the course?'

'No,' said Ann.

'Then you'd better get back to work.'

Jenny had helped Ann Mallon, then she managed to lose herself in more work for a few hours. And she had been with Mike. But when it was time to go home she found herself still depressed. And Mike had to stay behind for an extra couple of hours, there was a case he was needed for.

'I'll be all right,' she told him. 'I'll get a taxi home.'

She had determined to use taxis as much as possible. No way was she going to have Mike dancing attendance on her. He had his job to do. And, besides, she was determined to hang on to her independence. And she'd become quite friendly with a few of the taxi drivers.

Once at her block of flats she collected the mail from the box in the entrance hall. Typical medical mail—a vast number of promotional letters, catalogues and so on, most of which would go straight into the bin. She went up to the flat, put the letters on the kitchen table and made herself a cup of tea.

A quick sort through the letters and she'd start preparing the evening meal.

There was a letter from London, the address in a confident script. Jenny knew at once who it was from, and looked at it rather doubtfully.

Jenny's life at her London hospital had ended up a mess. She had come to this northern city to a new job, and in it had found a kind of therapy. Because she was so frantically busy she didn't have time to brood over what had happened. And she didn't want male companionship, which was a good thing because she didn't have time for it.

She had cut almost all ties with her old life. Only one old friend still kept in touch—Abby Ainsworth. Abby had been a support to her, a source of strength when she'd needed it. And they now wrote to each other about once a month.

She felt worse when she opened the letter. *I know you probably don't want to hear about him,* Abby wrote, *but perhaps you ought to know that Peter Murphy is back at the hospital. He's come back from America. He's got a big brassy wife who's a nurse and he seems thoroughly under her thumb. She doesn't like England and tells him all the time. Peter's got fat and is idle and whines all the time about the poor equipment we have here. You had a lucky escape from him. He's never once mentioned you...* The rest of the letter was pleasant and gossipy but Jenny was just not in the mood.

For a while she stayed by the window, staring at the passing ships. Then she went to the kitchen and slowly prepared the evening meal.

Mike arrived a couple of hours later. He kissed her, then immediately realised something was wrong. 'Are you still worried about the meeting with Spenser, sweetheart?'

She shook her head, silently passed him the letter. He read it. 'Peter Murphy was the man you had trouble with?'

'He was. Even though I hated him I used to think about him a lot. But recently—since I met you—I've stopped. You've wiped him out. In my mind I can put the two of you side by side, compare you. And I wonder how I ever could have fancied him.'

Mike led her into the sitting room, helped her out of the wheelchair and placed her easily on the couch. Then he sat next to her, put an arm round her. 'I knew he existed but you've never talked about him,' he said. 'Is now a good time perhaps?'

Perhaps it was a good time. Perhaps she could lay her ghosts.

'Well, he was fanciable,' she said. 'At least I thought he was at the time. He was a bit older, he was a doctor, he made a play for me and we finished up going out together. Then we lived together. We shared the costs of a flat in London.'

Jenny shook her head. 'Mike, I thought we were happy together. But it wasn't like with you. I just didn't know what happiness was. We never talked about marriage but—for me at least—it was a vaguely understood thing.'

His arm was still round her, his voice encouraging. 'So what happened?'

'I was doing an MA in midwifery, the one that

enabled me to come here, as well as working full-time as a midwife. Peter got the offer of a four-year contract in America and he wanted to start at once, wanted me to go with him. I said I wanted to wait nine months and finish my course. I'd completed two years of it already and it was the hardest work I'd ever done. He said it wasn't important. He needed someone to look after him in America. He needed me now, I wasn't to be selfish. He wanted me to drop everything for him.'

'Sounds like a man who knows his own mind,' said Mike, 'even if he doesn't care for anyone else's.'

'Quite. Well, I said I'd finish my course and then come out to him. And he got very nasty. I think then I started to wonder about him. But then I had a fort-night away, a specialised bit of training up in Birmingham. I tried to phone him and couldn't get through. And when I came back he had gone. He'd emptied all his stuff out of the flat. Taken some of my things. The place was dirty and he'd left me with all the bills. Just a scrawled note that since we couldn't get on he thought a clean break best. Not even a forwarding address.'

'Did you ever hear from him again?'

'Obviously he didn't want me to get in touch. But I got a home telephone number for him with the help of someone in the hospital office. And I phoned him. A woman answered, asked me if I was the pathetic little thing that had been hanging on to him, he'd told her all about me. Mike, this was after only three weeks! And she said I had to forget him, that they were together now.'

'You had a lucky escape,' Mike said after a while.

'Yes. I can see that now. But I can't forget that I thought we were happy. And we were, until he didn't get his own way.'

'Are you worried that that will happen to us?'

'Of course not! But I'm scared. I wonder that if…if things don't go well, and I'm in a wheelchair for the rest of my life, in time you might feel trapped.'

'It won't happen,' he said. 'You've brought me more happiness than I thought possible. And it's you I love—all of you, not just your legs.'

Jenny managed a weak smile. 'Well, I still want my own way. We wait.'

The physiotherapist had told her that after a while in the wheelchair she was likely to feel depressed but it would pass. She had had one episode of depression immediately after being discharged, but now the depression seemed to return. As a midwife, she had met many cases of postnatal depression, knew it was apparently without cause, and in time that, too, usually passed. But this knowledge didn't help her. Her world remained grey.

But she wouldn't give in! She was tough. Still, she wondered just how much she was fooling Mike.

Four days later she and Mike were invited to dinner with Sue, Harry and Sam. 'I'm going to enjoy this,' she told Mike, 'and we'll have to have them back here soon. You can cook something Mexican again.'

'Can I wear my sombrero and serape again?'

'No,' she said.

She had hoped that the anticipation of the meal would cheer her up. But it didn't. And she still couldn't hide what she was feeling from Mike. 'We don't have to go if you're not up to it,' he said gently. 'You know they'll understand.'

'I'm not going to give way to it,' she said fiercely. 'I've got to fight. I'll be all right once I get there.'

So she took particular care as she prepared for the evening. She wore a cream trouser suit she had bought with Sue, and she wore the green medallion Mike had given her. And her efforts were not in vain. The evening was a success and she found herself enjoying every minute.

As a special treat Sam was allowed to stay up for a while and have his own place at the table. Jenny had come to love him. She had wondered...just wondered...what it would be like to have a child of her own.

Harry told them of his experiences overseas, what medicine was like in the army. He and Mike compared notes on trying to treat people who had no knowledge of English. Sue talked about life in A and E. It was a good evening.

The phone rang and Sue went out to answer it. She came back, a doubtful expression on her face, and gave the portable handset to Jenny. 'It's for you,' she said. 'It's your surgeon, Mr Spenser.'

The others at the table stood, made to leave so Jenny could make her call in private. Impatiently she waved them to sit down. She had no secrets from her friends.

'I'm sorry to interrupt your social gathering,' Mr Spenser said apologetically. 'In fact, I've been phoning around to try to find you. You remember I said I wanted to show your case notes to an American professor? Well, he was very interested. He's come back up here with me for a couple of days. Could you—would you like him to examine you tomorrow morning? It's your choice but I think it a very good idea.'

'Of course he can examine me.'

'Things might be progressing a bit faster than I had thought,' Mr Spenser said. 'I'll see you in my rooms at nine tomorrow.' He rang off.

Jenny told the others what she had just heard. 'What does it mean?' asked Sue.

'I'm frightened,' said Jenny. 'I don't know whether to be happy or worried.'

Mike put his arm around her. 'Everything will be all right,' he said.

But the atmosphere had changed. They talked about what might or might not happen, agreed they had no facts. And then they left rather early, Jenny promising to phone as soon as she had any news.

They went to bed as soon as they got back to the flat. 'Put your arms around me and just hold me,' said Jenny. 'I want you to just hold me.'

In the night, when she woke, she found his arms still around her.

This time Mike insisted on coming with her. They made arrangements to cancel their work and went to see Mr Spenser together. And they met the American professor.

Jenny liked Professor Dunkel. He was the complete opposite of the tall thin Mr Spenser. He was short, broad, with massive shoulders. He wore a bowtie—with a Union Jack on it! With a great grin he told her that he wore it to remind him he was in a foreign country.

'I gather you're a midwife, so I can talk to you,' he said. 'You know the score. And this must be Dr Donovan. Aren't you the lucky one to be engaged to a gorgeous creature like this?'

Not a British professor, Jenny thought with a secret grin.

'Now, I'd like you to be looked at and pulled and prodded and so on again. I know you've just been through all this with Mr Spenser here, but I really want to see for myself. That OK? There's a nurse waiting for you next door.'

'Of course,' said Jenny.

It seemed to be a very similar examination to the one she had had before with Mr Spenser. Perhaps the professor spent more time touching her legs, constantly referring to the illuminated X-rays on the wall and the MRI and CT scans. Then he smiled and said, 'That wasn't too bad, was it? Get dressed again and I'll go and have a couple of words with Mr Spenser. We'll be in to see you.'

She sat with Mike. They held hands but she just didn't feel like talking. After about a quarter of an hour, Mr Spenser and Professor Dunkel came in to see them. They looked unusually solemn.

Mr Spenser spoke first. 'This ultimately must be your decision. I've already explained that perhaps in time things might improve in your legs. But they might not. Another operation would mean another stay in hospital, more pain and discomfort. However, I've conferred with Professor Dunkel here, we've reviewed your case notes and he suggests that an operation might be a good idea. In America he's developed a new technique which is not yet available in this country, he might be able to restore movement to your legs. He is here and he's willing to demonstrate the technique to me. But you must decide if you want to try it. The operation would be performed jointly by the Professor and myself.'

'One thing, Jenny,' the Professor said. 'I think we can do it. But if we're unsuccessful you might be a lot worse than you already are.'

'Could I wake up even more paralysed?'

'It's unlikely. It's not entirely impossible.'

'When would you want to do it?' Jenny asked.

'I have to get back to the States. So in two days' time.'

Jenny looked at Mike, who nodded. 'I'll arrange sick leave,' said Jenny. 'I don't need time to think about it. I'll have it done.'

He'd tried not to show it, but for some time now Mike had been worried about Jenny. She was still depressed, still low. She said nothing as they made their way back to her department. When he tried to be cheerful, said there was hope now, she merely snapped, 'Nothing at all has changed.' And when she got to her room, she said that she'd rather he didn't call round for lunch that day. She had a lot of work to get through.

She didn't even seem to be excited—or afraid—when she realised that her fate would be settled in just two days' time. It seemed it was just a minor irritation in an already dreary world. He hated it when she was this way, but there was nothing that he could do.

And he knew that deep down she was terrified.

He was terrified himself. If the worst happened, he did not know how she would cope with the prospect of being in a wheelchair for the rest of her life.

One thing he did know, one thing he was absolutely certain of—wheelchair or not, he wanted to be with her. For the rest of his life.

Could he convince her of that? He knew her doubts. He remembered his earlier uneasy suspicion that if she was told her condition was incurable she would refuse to marry him. Out of love and regard for him. She wouldn't want him to be tied to a woman who was condemned to live her life in a wheelchair. And however much he protested that he wanted to marry her anyway, she would ignore him.

And there was another thing, perhaps a matter of male pride. If he waited until after the operation and it was a success and then he asked her to marry him, she might wonder. Would he have asked her had she still been in a wheelchair?

Mike found himself getting angry. All he had to do was wait, there was nothing he could *do*. And he hated waiting, feeling powerless.

Two days to go. Then he grinned to himself. A lot could happen in two days.

Jenny felt that all the heart had gone out of her. She knew what it was, of course. Depression, a reaction—possibly physiological—to stress. But knowing what it was didn't make it any easier to bear. She knew that she could ask for antidepressant drugs, they'd worked for her before. But she wouldn't. She could hang on for a few days more.

And then there was Mike. She knew she was loved, knew he loved her. But she just couldn't show it. And she also knew that Mike was as terrified as she was. She wanted to reach out to him, to give him comfort and take it from him. But she couldn't. And at the moment he seemed to have more work on than usual, was preoccupied with something. Well, time would tell.

The operation was scheduled for two o'clock on Friday afternoon. Jenny was asked to go into hospital on Thursday evening for pre-op observations and preparations. Mike came in with her. She was given a side ward to herself again. Quite early—and very properly—the sister came in and shooed Mike out.

'I'll see you tomorrow morning?' Jenny asked anxiously. 'You will call in?'

Mike smiled. 'Oh, yes. You'll certainly see me tomorrow morning.'

Jenny was given a sedative, went to sleep quickly.

\* \* \*

She had no breakfast, of course, and nothing to drink as she was going to have a general anaesthetic. But a smiling nurse came in and helped her wash, gave her something to rinse out her mouth. Then she seemed to spend rather a lot of time tidying the room, smoothing the sheets and so on. And something seemed to be amusing her. Jenny just tried to concentrate on her book.

Jenny frowned. There seemed to be something of a ruckus outside her room. There were more footsteps than there should have been, the murmur of voices. What was going on? Finally the nurse glanced at her watch. 'I must be going,' she said. 'I hope it's all wonderful for you.'

Wonderful? An odd word to use about an operation. The nurse gave a conspiratorial grin, opened the door and slipped out.

The door remained open. Carelessly, Jenny looked up—and her mouth opened with astonishment. There was Mike—but in full morning dress? He looked magnificent. Dark trousers, a light grey frock coat, a rich red cravat over a gleaming white shirt. 'What the…?' asked Jenny.

He stepped into the room, bent to kiss her. 'This will be the shortest engagement in history,' he said. 'I already know you want to marry me so I'm not going to waste time asking you.'

He took her unresisting hand and on her third finger slipped the jade and diamond ring she had so much liked in the jewellery shop. 'Now we're engaged, we can get married. This will have to be in a bit of a hurry, I gather you've got some business this afternoon.'

'Mike, we can't get married here and now! It's just not possible.'

She recognised the expression on his face at once. Mike Donovan was going to have what he wanted— and no one had better get in the way!

'Oh, yes, it is possible. Now, we can have another ceremony later in a church, and get some official piece of paper and have a big party afterwards. But we're getting married right now! The hospital chaplain, the Reverend Madeleine Hall, is a lovely woman. I went to see her, explained the problem, and she says she can perform the full service for us— she just can't do the official paperwork at such short notice.'

'So we won't quite really be married?'

'Yes, we will. Not in the eyes of the law, perhaps, but certainly in the eyes of everyone who matters. That's you, me and all our friends and family.'

He kissed her again. 'See you in ten minutes.' And he was gone.

Into the room trooped Sue and Lucy Stephens and Maria Wyatt, two of her favourite ex-students. All were giggling. They looked elegant, wore hats, expensive outfits, corsages. Behind them came Linda, the girl at the salon who did Jenny's hair. And over Sue's arms was draped a length of white silk.

'This is the wedding dress you picked,' Sue said. 'Remember, when we looked at that parade in that store? They had it in your size. So out of bed and we'll help you on with it. And Linda here has come to fix your hair and make-up. Can't have a bare-faced bride, can we?'

'What's happening?' asked the bewildered Jenny.

'You're getting married. Happiest day of a girl's life. Well, it was for me and it will be for you.'

'But he hasn't asked me! I haven't said yes! He just charged in and put the ring on my finger!' Jenny looked down at her hand and said absently, 'But it's nice, isn't it?'

'You can't change your mind now,' said Sue, conveniently ignoring the fact that Jenny hadn't made it up in the first place. 'All the arrangements have been made. And if anyone can make you happy it's my little brother. You love him, don't you?'

'Well, yes,' said Jenny. 'But I thought—'

'Off with that nightie,' said Sue. 'And, Maria, can you fetch in the flowers?'

It was a wedding dress for walking down an aisle, but it didn't look too bad in a wheelchair. And Mike had said that she could have another ceremony later. She was quickly eased out of bed, the dress put on her. Then Linda wrapped a sheet around her shoulders and fixed her hair and make-up, Then the cap and veil. Lucy fetched a large mirror.

'You look absolutely gorgeous,' Sue said, a quiver in her voice.

'I know,' said Jenny. Well, she did look gorgeous.

Outside she could hear the shuffling of more feet, the murmur of more voices. She seemed to be carried along by a force she couldn't recognise, as if she had no will of her own. Then she realised she rather liked it. Then she realised something else. The blackness of the previous few days had left her. She was her own self again.

'I'm matron of honour,' Sue said, 'and Maria and Lucy are your two bridesmaids. We're altering things a bit, feminine solidarity and all that. I'm also going to give you away. Well, why not? Sam's outside, he's not quite sure about his page-boy outfit but he's getting used to it.' She handed Jenny a bouquet. 'These are your flowers. Now we can start. Reverend, we're ready!'

Jenny had met Madeleine Hall before and very much liked her. She was always ready to come to comfort patients, occasionally had baptised a child when the parents had wanted it done at once. Now she walked into the room, a beaming smile on her face. She was wearing her vestments.

'You've no idea how much I enjoy weddings,' she told Jenny. 'Especially when I'm in charge. I was so pleased when Mike came to see me, told me that you'd made up your mind.'

'He did it for me,' said Jenny.

'Now, I'm afraid I've got to make you understand. This is not a legal wedding, it's a ceremony of blessing. But we'll use the complete wedding service, and as far as I'm concerned you'll be married in God's eyes—and in your own. Are you ready?'

Jenny closed her eyes for a moment. Then she opened them and said, 'I'm ready.'

Sue went to the door, signalled. And Mike walked in again.

Jenny thought her heart would burst with love.

He'd done all this for her! Now she knew why he'd seemed so preoccupied over the past two days, why she'd seen so little of him. And it was so like him! Cut red tape. Go for what you want. And she knew now that it was what she wanted, too.

He walked to her, looked down at her. She lifted her veil and he bent to kiss her cheek.

'I took a risk,' he said, 'but I wanted to make you happy.'

'I'm happy,' she told him. 'Happier than I've been in months.'

'In that case, meet my best man and your page-boy.'

Behind Mike was Harry, looking incredibly smart in his uniform and carrying a now happy Sam in white shirt, velvet shorts and a black bow-tie.

'If you'd like to stand in front of me,' said Madeleine.

Then the room filled with more people than Jenny could have imagined it holding. There were Mr Spenser and Professor Dunkel, both in scrubs. There were nurses from the wards, her students. There were people from the university.

'Dearly beloved,' Madeleine began, 'we are gathered here together...'

Jenny had been to weddings before, knew the service as well as anyone. But as she listened to those familiar words, they became new again, and magic. 'To love and honour... With this ring I thee wed...'

It was a short service but she loved it. He had picked the wedding ring, plain and simple, she liked that, too. And he had bought her a ring to give to him. That was clever of him, she thought. How had he known that she'd want him to wear her ring?

'I pronounce you man and wife,' Madeleine said. 'You may kiss the bride.'

Mike kissed her. She was married.

Then the ward sister bustled in, a grin on her face. 'Right, this is a hospital, not a chapel. All of you out, Dr Donovan, you can spend a five-minute honeymoon with your wife. Then you're out, too.'

Cheerfully, the crowd started to move out. Sue bent over Jenny. 'Your corsage,' she whispered. 'Pull the rubber band off and it'll split in two.'

'So?'

'You've got two unmarried bridesmaids. I arranged it specially.'

Jenny smiled. She pulled off the band, separated the two parts of the corsage. 'Lucy, Maria,' she called.

Her bridesmaids turned, each caught the expertly thrown flowers. 'You'll be next,' Jenny threatened.

And then she was alone with Mike.

'You always get your own way,' she whispered to him.

'Not my way. Our way. I wanted you to have this operation knowing that I'd be waiting for you, however it goes. And I'm the happiest man on earth right now.'

He kissed her again. 'I'll be waiting for you, Mrs Donovan,' he said.

Two nurses came in when he left, carefully helped her off with the dress and then washed and prepped her. This was something she had done herself, she knew the procedure. But time now seemed to pass like a dream. An operation—no trouble. Mike would be waiting for her afterwards.

The anaesthetist came in to see her, did his own checks and seemed quite happy. Then there was the ride to the theatre on a trolley. She saw Mike in the corridor, managed to wave to him.

The theatre anteroom. The IV was connected. And then instant blackness.

Jenny came swimming back to consciousness. There were people around her but she'd rather go back to sleep. Perhaps she ought to tell someone. She was going to have an anaesthetic and it hadn't worked. 'I'm still awake,' she mumbled. 'I can't go into Theatre yet.'

Softly, a voice said, 'You've been to Theatre. It's all done.'

Slowly, she woke up.

He was by her bed. Mike. She was married to him now. He took her hand, slipped two rings onto her finger. She'd had to take them off for the operation but she wanted them back on now.

His voice was apparently careless.

'Love you, sweetheart,' he said. 'I've been out to the travel agents, got a couple of ideas for our honeymoon. In a month or two. I thought we might go to Argentina.'

'Why Argentina?'

'It'll be carnival time. People dance every night. In the streets, in their homes, in hotels.'

'Dancing?'

'Try to wriggle your toes.' She did. And she could!

'I've just talked to Professor Dunkel, Mr Spenser. It went well. In four months' time you'll be working, walking, running, dancing. Fancy that, Mrs Donovan?'

'I fancy anything with you,' she said.

She was drowsy, she knew she was going to sleep again. But she felt his gentle kiss. And as her eyes closed, she smiled. Her future would be so happy— with Mike.

MILLS & BOON®

0205/03b

*Live the emotion*

# _Medical_
## romance™

### *THE DOCTOR'S PREGNANCY SURPRISE by Kate Hardy*

*(London City General)*

Dr Holly Jones has never recovered from the shock of
losing David Neave's baby – nor from the way he
disappeared from her life. Years later they find
themselves working together in A&E, and as their long-
held secrets come bubbling to the surface they begin to
renew their very special bond. Until Holly discovers
she's pregnant again!

### THE CONSULTANT'S SECRET SON *by Joanna Neil*

Dr Allie Russell is managing the best she can – juggling
her work in A&E and Search & Rescue with her two-
year-old son. Then Nathan Brewster arrives back in her
life as the new A&E consultant. He doesn't know he's
Matty's father, and Allie wants to keep it that way. But
as she and Nathan draw closer again, it's only a matter
of time before he discovers the truth!

### NURSE IN RECOVERY *by Dianne Drake*

Charge nurse Anna Wells's life has been shattered by
an accident. She needs someone very dedicated and
special to help her put the pieces back together...
someone like brilliant Rehabilitation doctor Mitch
Durant. But Mitch is burnt out, the last thing he needs
is another patient – until he sees Anna and realises
she's a challenge he just has to take on...

## On sale 4th March 2005

*Available at most branches of WHSmith, Tesco, ASDA, Martins,*
*Borders, Eason, Sainsbury's and all good paperback bookshops.*

*Visit www.millsandboon.co.uk*

# FREE

## 4 BOOKS AND A SURPRISE GIFT!

We would like to take this opportunity to thank you for reading this
Mills & Boon® book by offering you the chance to take FOUR more
specially selected titles from the Medical Romance™ series absolutely
FREE! We're also making this offer to introduce you to the benefits of
the Reader Service™—

- ★ **FREE home delivery**
- ★ **FREE gifts and competitions**
- ★ **FREE monthly Newsletter**
- ★ **Books available before they're in the shops**
- ★ **Exclusive Reader Service offers**

Accepting these FREE books and gift places you under no obligation
to buy; you may cancel at any time, even after receiving your free
shipment. Simply complete your details below and return the entire
page to the address below. You don't even need a stamp!

**YES!** Please send me 4 free Medical Romance books and a surprise
gift. I understand that unless you hear from me, I will receive 6
superb new titles every month for just £2.69 each, postage and packing
free. I am under no obligation to purchase any books and may cancel
my subscription at any time. The free books and gift will be mine to
keep in any case.

M5ZEE

Ms/Mrs/Miss/Mr.......................................Initials ...............................
                                                           **BLOCK CAPITALS PLEASE**

Surname ....................................................................................................

Address ....................................................................................................

...................................................................................................................

.......................................................Postcode ...................................

Send this whole page to:
The Reader Service, FREEPOST CN81, Croydon, CR9 3WZ

# WIN a romantic weekend in PARiS

*To celebrate Valentine's Day we are offering you the chance to WIN one of 3 romantic weekend breaks to Paris.*

Imagine you're in Paris; strolling down the Champs Elysées, pottering through the Latin Quarter or taking an evening cruise down the Seine. Whatever your mood, Paris has something to offer everyone.

For your chance to make this dream a reality simply enter this prize draw by filling in the entry form below:

Name _____

Address _____

_____ Tel no: _____

## Closing date for entries is 30th June 2005

### Please send your entry to:

**Valentine's Day Prize Draw**
**PO Box 676, Richmond, Surrey, TW9 1WU**